THE SWITCH

by

ZAK JANE KEIR

CHIMERA

The Switch first published in 1997 by
Chimera Publishing Ltd
PO Box 152
Waterlooville
Hants
PO8 9FS

Printed and bound in Great Britain by Caledonian
International Book Manufacturing Ltd., Glasgow

New authors welcome

THE SWITCH

Zak Jane Keir

To Gwenn and Liz, fellow Cherry babies. To Pam for picking up on a dream, and Mad Man Martin for obvious reasons.

ONE: Love in an Elevator

The cane whistled through the air and landed with an audible bite. Poppy Ryanson gave a sigh of pure release, unclenched her hands and began to cry. The fourth stroke landed precisely on the site of the third, making her yelp aloud, raising herself onto tiptoes and tossing her long red hair from side to side.

"I'll run away, you beast," she cried suddenly, and the cane abruptly halted its fifth descent.

"I'd find you. No matter where you ran, I'd find you," Max Ryanson replied, and she heard him toss the cane indifferently away. She relaxed, thinking the punishment over for the time being, and then began to squeal again as a volley of hard, open-handed smacks landed on her throbbing, burning rear.

The whipping block to which he'd tied her was one he'd made himself: a simple folding construction with a well-padded leather top and rings on the base of each leg to tie her ankles and wildly flailing hands. Now and again, he would put her on her honour to be still, held in place only by the force of his will and her own desire to surrender to it. Usually, she would comply, though once she had received her punishment in such utter, submissive silence that he had halted the thorough strapping he was giving her to make sure she was not in genuine distress. When the upward curve of her mouth betrayed her, she had received fifteen hard ones from the thinnest, stingiest cane for sheer dumb insolence, and what a joy that had been!

On another occasion, she had chosen her moment, catapulted herself to a standing position and cavorted round the room like a frisky pony, fit and agile enough to avoid Max's grasp for some fifteen minutes, even though she had been masturbating furiously for the last five. When he caught her, he didn't beat her again, but wrestled her firmly to the floor and, holding her in place with one hard hand on the back of her neck, had dilated and greased her with the fingers of the other hand before lubricating his angrily pulsing member with her vaginal juices and taking her anally, so that her orgasm was almost agonisingly delayed.

Their sessions in the Punishment Room were never the same twice, which may have been one of the reasons for the blissful survival of the marriage between a dignified forty-year-old architect and a twenty-four-year-old red-headed scamp who had never held down a job for more than a fortnight in her life.

Now, as she knelt at his feet to perform the oral service he had requested with a single brisk hand gesture, Poppy looked up at her husband with the unquenchable spark of mischief in her big brown eyes and said: "I will, you know. I'll run away. I'll run away for the rest of the summer, and you won't be able to find me until I'm ready to come home."

Max, who was, in fact, half an inch shorter than his wife, with side-parted brown hair and powerful, long-fingered hands, looked down into her beautiful, wicked little face, shaking his head.

"Little slut, you know what happened the last time you tried. I know you won't be able to manage without me, that you won't last more than a day on your own. In fact, if you manage to stay away, where I can't find you, for more than a week, I'll buy you a new Porsche. No - !" for she seemed on the verge of protesting, "Permission to speak withdrawn. That is my promise to you and that is where this discussion ends. Now use that slutty little mouth for what you're best at and take my seed. Make me orgasm, bitch, and maybe I'll let you rub yourself off."

Elsewhere, some days later, a red-haired woman with slanting blue eyes and a lush, full-bodied figure, a woman who had not yet met Poppy Ryanson, had spent the past few hours either sleeping or counting her blessings. Stephanie Ames, author of screenplays for five successful horror films, beloved and occasionally stern mistress of two adoring, gorgeous men on a regular basis, had the rest of the summer to do with as she pleased.

Now she was beginning to wake up, aware of the moist touch of a mouth on her left nipple, sucking, tugging slightly, with a minimal scrape of teeth over the little bud, just enough to bring it springing into hardness, swelling with the early stirrings of a full-blown passionate pleasure. Stephanie loved having her nipples nibbled.

She didn't open her eyes, not just yet. She lay very still, letting her mind come fully alive as her nerve-endings woke, reveling in the dawning sensations; a gathering moisture between her legs, a slow, steady throb of tension in the depths of her vulva, and through it all the sweet, determined suckling, the gentle tickling of beard hairs against her breast. Beard. Paul, then. At last, she opened her eyes and smiled.

"About time too, Redhead," he said, raising himself on one elbow and grinning at her. Her well-muscled Viking blond, with a sinful angel's face and maybe the dirtiest mind in the whole South East. Well, one of the dirtiest minds, anyway.

"What time is it?" she asked, rubbing her eyes.

"Seven o' clock."

"In the morning? For fuck's sake, Paul!"

"Seven p.m., Red, get with it. You said you wanted to wake up before eight, so ..."

"So it's seven o' clock. Can you think of any good reason for waking me up an hour before I said I wanted to wake up?"

Her eyes were fully focussed now, and she could see that Paul was naked, stripped of everything but the tiger's-eye pendant he wore on a thong around his neck. Her own teeth marks from the night before stood out against his fair skin, and from the curly hair at his groin his cock reared up, strong and proud, dark with excitement.

"I reckon that's a good enough reason," she said, giggling as she reached for him. She had been sleeping, as usual, in the middle of the big double bed, having retreated there dizzy with exhaustion three or four hours ago. They'd been partying the night before, and playing games of their own until dawn - no wonder she had been sleepy. Now, though, she felt refreshed, revitalized, and more than ready for another helping.

Both her nipples were erect, in little sharp, pale fawn points, thrusting forward, and when she rubbed her thighs together she could feel the wetness in her quim, the hollow ache that needed to be filled.

Wrapping her fingers round Paul's erection she squeezed experimentally, moving the loose skin over the hardness, and heard his breathing quicken. He was half-crouching, half-kneeling beside her, bending over so his mouth could find her breasts again, sucking and biting on the swollen fawn areolae as she caressed him. She raised her knees, moving them apart to allow his free hand access to her sex, and her labia parted with a faint but audible squelch as his fingers made one determined thrust, then began to burrow in a gentle fashion, ploughing the furrow again and again, opening her wider, paying the perfect amount of attention to the little pearl of her clit, tantalizing her almost unbearably.

She let go of his cock so she could take him by the shoulder-blades, inexorably moving him on top of her, opening her legs even further as she pulled him down and drew him in, running her hands down his back to squeeze his buttocks as she welcomed him inside herself. Three times she felt him push hard into her, that slippery firm motion she adored, and then he paused for a moment, smiling at her, grey eyes slitted in a languorous, cat-like smugness so that she reached up and locked her fingers at the base of his neck, bringing his mouth down onto hers and plunging her tongue in between his teeth, swiveling her hips as she did, making her desire and her intention utterly plain. She felt him laugh against her lips and then he raised his body, tilted himself and powered down, fucking her so deliciously that her legs came up and wrapped around his waist almost without any conscious control on her behalf. He was moving pretty quickly now, supporting himself on his forearms, twisting his neck and shoulders now andagain to bite or kiss her face or throat. She clung with her pussy muscles, clenching and relaxing, rotating her hips a little, just enough to boost the stimulation of her clitoris as their bodies ground together. Heat was speeding through her, a pulsing warm sensation radiating out from her vulva, up through her body and down the inside of each thigh. Paul let out a soft, shuddering moan and thrust down really hard, paused, froze, and gave one final, quivering lunge, just as the powerful spasms of her pussy overcame her.

It was a quarter to three in the morning, and Stephanie was beginning to feel thoroughly out of sorts and irritable. Usually, a night in the Black Light fetish club would energize her, stimulate her senses, provoke her to even greater heights of sexual excess, but nothing had been working for her tonight. Maybe it had been a mistake to go alone, refusing Paul's offer to accompany her, not bothering to ring Alex and persuade him to come out and play rather than working that night; perhaps her vague impulse to find new prey was sheer greed. For whatever reason, the club tonight had been full of out-of-towners, idiots showing off in their first pair of cheap PVC trousers, and running away at the merest suggestion of a little fun in the whipping room. Stephanie liked to chastise, but only when the victims were either willing or seductively defiant; these wimps weren't worth the strength of her arm.

Oh, and here came that silly redheaded bitch again, prancing along the corridor that divided bar from dance floor with another couple of meatheads in tow. Steph was proud of her own red hair, liking the way it marked her out in the crowd, and she wasn't pleased to have her uniqueness compromised by this squealing, giggling, bouncing brat. It wasn't as if the other was even properly dressed for the club.

Stephanie herself was wearing scarlet rubber trousers tucked into scarlet cowboy boots, a black lace bra top and a silver alien-head pendant. Clipped to her studded leather belt were a paddle and a small but spiteful rubber cat o' nine tails.

The other redhead was wearing a brief, clingy dress of turquoise Lycra and silver tap shoes, and carrying a white PVC shoulder bag that looked heavy enough to overbalance her. In fact, it did exactly that as she drew level with Stephanie, and when one of her companions rather over-enthusiastically tried to steady her, the brief skirt flew up to demonstrate an absence of panties. Steph raised an eyebrow - not so much at the lack of underwear but at what else that lack revealed; the marks of a well-whipped arse. Her dislike of the girl dwindled rapidly as she

10

contemplated the kind of beating that would leave such lingering, tell-tale traces. She only rarely got the opportunity to spank or thrash another girl, but had thoroughly enjoyed such opportunities as had come her way.

Heading back towards the bar, Stephanie half-turned for a final look at the other, who had paused in the alcove that marked the end of the corridor and was engaged in animated discussion with her two companions, clearly demanding something or other. It didn't appear that her wish was going to be granted, and Stephanie suddenly felt sorry for her. Miss No-Knickers probably wanted either a good fuck or a good hiding, and had chosen the wrong boys to ask about it. They wouldn't know what they were missing, of course - the joy of chastising a genuinely naughty submissive, one who relished the pain and yet defied the inflictor of it, the best of all possible scenes ... Stephanie pushed back her hair and went on her way. One more drink and then she was going to call it a night. Maybe Alex would still be awake - he would have finished his shift with the cab firm by now, and if he hadn't taken himself off to one of his favourite seedy drinking dens, perhaps he would be in the mood for a taste of Stephanie's own personal brand of intoxication.

The Black Light was being held in one of its most popular venues, a hastily-converted warehouse basement in West London. Stephanie, having utterly given up on the prospect of anything occurring to enliven her night within its confines, was waiting, jacket loosely round her shoulders, in the dark alcove which housed the rickety lift that provided the only means of entry and exit to the club, unless one were healthy or masochistic enough to climb the two hundred stairs to street level. Most people had gone home, or were clearly determined to be swept out with the fag ends when the bar finally closed, and

Stephanie leaned back against the wall for a moment, closing her eyes and breathing deeply.

The clatter of heels roused her, and it was with mixed feelings that she saw the other redhead rapidly approaching. The girl's mouth was set in sulky lines, and her whole demeanour suggested a deep and thoroughgoing petulance. As she drew level with the protruding wall of the lift housing, she suddenly loosed a vicious kick at the paintwork, taking Stephanie by surprise.

"Steady on, what's the matter with you?"

"I'm fucked off with the world," the other replied. She was rubbing her toe down the back of her calf as though already regretting that kick, and Stephanie struggled to keep back a smile as, with a creak and a groan, the lift arrived.

When the doors strained open to let them in, Poppy was able to get a good look at the other girl, and to calculate how much she liked what she saw. Her head had been spinning with half-formed plans of varying implausibility all night, but something was finally beginning to crystallise. Her mood swiftly improved, but there was a powerful awareness that she would need to handle this interaction very carefully if she were to get her own way.

The other girl, older and slightly taller than her, had stepped into the lift, and was clearly waiting for her to do the same. Poppy took one fast shallow breath and deliberately dropped her handbag so that it burst open as it hit the floor, spilling make-up, matchboxes, small change and tissues both in and out of the lift. She bent down, not too fast and not too slow, and began to pick up her possessions, already proud of herself for succeeding with this early move. The other girl couldn't do anything but assist, as her things were equally distributed inside and outside the lift, making any attempt to move it upwards

12

extremely difficult to do without causing a scene.

Poppy kept up a lively monologue as she retrieved lipsticks, coins, and cigarette cards, all about what a lousy night she was having, what a lousy week she'd had, and wasn't everything just a bastard? The older redhead's hands moved with a sure competence, and though she hadn't displayed anything other than a weary resignation at first, Poppy could tell the other's eyes were lingering on her body as she stooped and scrabbled around.

"You really aren't having much fun, are you?" she said as Poppy stuffed the final handful of flyers into the battered old bag.

"I saw you earlier - it didn't look like those two guys were a lot of use to you."

Poppy blinked, wondering for one awful moment if she had miscalculated again. There was something very knowing in the other's manner - but she was smiling now, smiling in a slow and rather promising way. She turned and pushed the button that would get the lift to rise, then turned back, still with that unsettling smile.

"Mind you," she drawled, "I would have thought you'd been smacked enough for one day. Looked to me like you had a lovely warm bum already."

Poppy blushed, aware that she did it prettily, the idea coming to her fully formed now.

"But I'm a very bad girl," she said, looking the other full in the face. "I need a lot of punishment, otherwise I get into awful trouble, because I'm just *so* naughty."

She had to do it fast to make it work, and she was going to give it her best try. She whipped off one of the silver shoes, flipped down the lift's control panel with her other hand, and smacked the heel of her shoe against the thing as hard as she could, cracking one of the old-fashioned glass knobs and breaking another right off. The lift gave an ominous groan and stopped, roughly halfway between

13

the basement and the ground.

Stephanie wasn't often lost for words, but she could barely believe her eyes as this lissome, lovely little bitch not only jammed the lift but absolutely trashed the controls. She was almost angry at the fact that she had now been let in for a long and inconvenient wait for rescue, but the sheer audacity of the girl's behaviour made it impossible for her to lose her temper properly.

When she finally found her voice, she was glad her first utterance was, as Paul would have put it, in keeping.

"I guess you haven't been spanked enough tonight, after all."

The brown eyes opened even wider, and a little pink tongue ran briefly over the pouty lower lip as the girl closed the panel again, stepped away from her handiwork and looked Steph in the eye.

"I did tell you I'm a naughty girl," she whispered.

Steph stretched, flexing her shoulders as she glanced around the confines of their musty metal cage. She shrugged her jacket off and tossed it into a corner.

"What's your name, girl?"

"Poppy, miss."

"You call me Madame. Madame Stephanie. Now bend over and clasp your ankles, you tiresome, troublesome, naughty little girl."

As Poppy did so, Stephanie neatly flicked up her little skirt, revealing those poor punished buttocks in all their glory. Newer cane marks were criss-crossed over old, and here and there were tiny, healing cuts from a well-plied whip or cat. Stephanie stroked the other girl's bottom, testing its heat with her hand. As the lift was stuffy and the August night warm, so was Poppy's flesh - but it would probably be considerate to prepare the girl for the sting of the paddle or the bite of the cat with a preliminary

14

spanking.

On the other hand, the little cow didn't really deserve much consideration, did she? Stephanie was tired, Stephanie had had other plans, and now she was stuck in this smelly metal box, all because of one selfish, naughty, hot-bottomed little slut. She unclipped the paddle, which was made of scarlet leather, and the size, if not quite the shape, of a plimsoll, and swung it once, firmly though not brutally, at the pert buttocks in front of her. The blow landed with a sharp snapping whack, and Poppy gasped but didn't move. Stephanie applied the paddle again, bringing up a bright red slap-mark on the left buttock, then matched it with another on the right, and one lower down, just at the point where the fleshy curve merged into the thigh.

"Are you sorry yet?" she asked sarcastically as this blow brought a little wail from her bent-over victim. The response was a naughty giggle and the words, "Course not."

Stephanie began to paddle Poppy's bottom in a steady, rhythmic manner, making each blow of roughly equal weight, turning that lovely arse to a glorious, glowing shade of red. After a while, Poppy was dancing, shifting her feet and jerking upwards with each resounding report, but she didn't let go of her ankles and she never said or did anything to suggest that the punishment was becoming unreasonably brutal. Oh, she was a joy to beat, that beautiful rear, so visibly responsive, the little moans and gasps she made and, best of all, that tiny, shiny trail of lubricating juice that was just becoming visible on the inside of her left thigh. Stephanie paused in her wielding of the paddle and inserted the flat of her hand between the trembling limbs, angling it upwards so her fingertips just brushed the hot, wet, swollen lips of Poppy's vagina.

"You dirty little pig," she hissed, wiping her hand

15

across the other's face. "You're wet. You filthy girl, to get sexually aroused when someone's giving you a good hard beating. How dare you enjoy this?"

"I'm not enjoying it, Madame," Poppy protested, still with a betraying hint of laughter in her voice. Stephanie sighed, theatrically.

"You won't enjoy the next bit, bitch," she threatened. A new idea had occurred to her, and she could feel her own vulva moistening and opening up.

"Tell me, Poppy-piglet, have you ever been spanked until you cry?"

Poppy waggled her bottom but said nothing. Stephanie looked again at the flushed, reddened orbs, so smooth, so sinful, and unclipped the whip, drawing it through the fingers of her other hand in a leisurely, menacing manner.

Crack!

The first lash fell slightly too far to the left, curling round to mark the soft curve of the hip.

Crack!

Stephanie corrected her aim and increased her force. Poppy was tensing her buttocks and clenching her thighs together, but she made no sound, and Steph was determined to draw one from her.

The strokes fell fast, and then faster, the vicious cracking of the nine-tailed whip sounding almost like gunfire, and Poppy gripped her ankles harder and harder as the burning, stinging pain increased. She blinked, her chest tensing with the effort of holding back the flood of threatening tears, savouring the moment, knowing how sweet would be the absolute surrender when it came. Abruptly, the blazing symphony ceased to be played on her bottom, and she let out a little grunt of surprise.

"Stand up," came the command, and she stumbled as she obeyed. Madame Stephanie took her by the shoulders and pushed her, quite roughly, up against the dull grey metal wall of the lift.

"You're up to something," she said, taking a grip of Poppy's chin. "There's something else you want, isn't there?" Poppy panicked for a moment, knew she had no option but to play along, and tried to nod her head, but found that her jaw was held too tightly. Her new mistress let her go, then slapped her sharply on the cheek.

"You don't want it badly enough," Stephanie said crossly. "You think you can just ask, and get, don't you? I don't know what it is you want, but you won't get it by fluttering your eyelashes at me. You'll have to convince me you want it."

Actually, Stephanie was surprising herself with every word and action. She loved to dominate, but she had never before hungered so badly for another's tears. The whole encounter had taken on a strange, surreal feeling of time-out-of-time, as though the lift's doors were a psychic barrier as well as a material one, between the two of them and the outside world. The link between Poppy and herself seemed far stronger than that of two girls who had fancied a little fun together, and she knew there was a strong likelihood that she would acquiesce with Poppy's desire, but only when she had made the other work for it. She slapped her again, and when Poppy gasped, she seized one of her nut-brown nipples and pinched it hard through the flimsy Lycra.

"I could do that to your clitty, couldn't I?" she taunted, and slapped Poppy's face again. Grabbing her arm, she whirled her round, bending her over her raised thigh and striking her buttocks with the flat of her hand, aiming for the areas worst marked by the whip. Poppy wriggled, so Steph hauled her upright, made her face the wall and held her by the scruff of her neck as she administered a wild spanking that made her own hand sting and throb. Poppy was clenching her fists and gasping, and Steph spanked her even harder.

"I won't stop till I see you cry!" she panted, and this final threat had the desired effect. Poppy tottered slightly and burst flamboyantly into tears. Steph turned her round again, letting her lean against the wall, nudged her thighs apart as she sobbed loudly, then swiftly inserted her index and middle fingers into Poppy's slit, rubbing her clit with her thumb. Still crying hard, Poppy orgasmed intensely over Stephanie's hand.

When she was done, and both the sobs and the shudders of her climax had subsided, Steph took the younger girl in her arms and lowered her gently down to the lift floor, holding her close and stroking her hair.

Poppy rocked blissfully against her former tormentor, a warm contentment filling her, turning her almost drowsy. She was roused from this state by the sound of an unfamiliar voice echoing down the lift shaft.

"All right in there? Yoo-Hoooooooo!"

"Yeah, we're here, we're fine!" Stephanie shouted. "How long before you can get us out?"

"About half an hour!" came the reply. Poppy swallowed hard, shifting her position. Half an hour meant she would have to make her move, and make it well. Stephanie had evidently noticed the change in her mood, because she tapped her on the shoulder more hesitantly than she would have done a few minutes earlier.

"What is it, little minx? It won't be that long, I shouldn't think."

Poppy took a deep breath, knowing that this was probably her last chance to pull off a truly spectacular scheme.

"I - I need your help," she said, carefully. "You see, I'm - Well, I need a place to hide."

"To hide," Steph echoed, and her face was suddenly too pale. "Has someone - is someone hurting you? I mean, what I did -" She was floundering, clearly distressed by what was going through her head, and Poppy felt a flash of guilt. She couldn't play on Stephanie's conscience like this - she liked her, and anyway, it wouldn't be right. Poppy liked to do mischief rather than cause emotional pain.

"No - I mean, I like being smacked, it's nothing to do with that. It's more of a game. I just need to get away for a few days, you see. I mean, I'm expected to be in one place and I - well I intend to be somewhere else."

Stephanie was still studying her, seriously. "Do you want to come home with me?" she asked, after a moment or two, and Poppy bit her lip.

"Not exactly. I mean, I already had a plan, sort of, about where to go, but then I saw you and I thought of something even better. You know - because we're both redheads."

"What the hell?"

It was all or nothing, and Poppy decided to gamble as hard as she could. Looking Stephanie full in the face, she said quietly, "I thought we could maybe pretend to be each other ... for a little while."

Steph's mouth opened wide and then shut again without emitting a word, but she didn't seem to be altogether appalled at the idea. There was just enough curiosity in her eyes for Poppy to continue.

"You see, I'm meeting this friend of mine who's going to let me hide at his, but if you went with him instead of me and I went to stay in your house, well -"

"Are you out of your bloody mind?" Stephanie interrupted, and Poppy subsided, biting her finger ends and gazing at the floor. Damn, she'd lost her chance. She should have known it was too much to ask, even though she had felt such startling closeness with the other, such a bond, even in the short space of time they had been together. It looked like she was all set for another embarrassing defeat.

Stephanie got up, and began to pace around the lift. The conniving little cow! What the hell was all this about? Of course her scheme was patently absurd, what on earth made her think that anyone would agree to sending a total stranger back to their house for an unspecified time?

"Don't you think my husband would notice if you showed up in bed instead of me? she snapped, and Poppy began to cry again, but this time without any enjoyment.

"You never said you had a husband," she sobbed, scrubbing her eyes with her fingers.

"Well it didn't exactly come up in conversation!"

Despite her better judgement, Steph felt a sudden pang of pity, and behind it, something else, some feeling of wild daring. She tried to quench it, but it wouldn't quit, the possibility opening up with irresistible appeal. Her most recent script, 'Hands of the Night', had been submitted - and paid for - a fortnight ago, and there would be no urgent work to be done until September. She liked her life, but weren't there times when she yearned to do something really daring? After all, shouldn't a true writer experience a bit of everything while she was young enough to do so?

Poppy was still crying, and Steph bent down to hug her. "Don't howl, kiddo, I haven't got a husband. It's just that it sounds like such a crazy idea - I mean, you smashed up the lift controls, what if you smashed up my flat?"

Poppy stared at her with drenched eyes, and suddenly began to scrabble around in her handbag. She pulled out a slim black purse, opened it and showed it to Steph. As well as a sheaf of banknotes, it contained a gold credit card in the name of Poppy A Ryanson. "Look, if anything gets damaged in your place, I'll pay for it! There's my name, and address, and everything, if you'll only help me!" she stammered.

Stephanie took the purse and looked at it thoughtfully. She thought of her small, neat flat, and how little value most of the contents really had. She thought of her currently fat bank account, and decided that her own credit card was staying with her - after all, she might want to do something daring, but there was a difference between daring and demented. She handed back the purse and ruffled the other girl's tangled red hair.

"All right, Poppy Ryanson, suppose I do swap lives with you for a while?"

At the very least, she thought, I might get a damn good screenplay out of this. I'd just have to turn one of us into a vampire or something. I reckon this break could do me good. Never mind the fact that an occasional act of wild lunacy tends to help a girl's reputation rather than hinder it in this line of business.

When the summoned engineer finally pried the lift doors open, at a quarter past four, it was beginning to get light, and the club manager had disappeared back into the bowels of his building. The two red-headed beauties thanked the engineer politely as they clambered out, and he felt a slight twinge from his groin at the sight of them.

I hope it wasn't too bad in there, he thought, and it occurred to him to imagine that he, too, had been trapped in the lift with the girls. Maybe they could have had an enjoyable time while they waited for someone to come and let them out. He allowed himself to picture himself lying flat on his back in the restricted space, with the taller of the two girls slowly peeling off her jeans to lower herself onto his erect, eager cock, accepting him fully and deeply inside herself while his tongue thrust and probed into the soft wet quim of the other, teasing the tiny nub of her clit and getting her creamy juices smeared all over his face.

Shaking his head, he forced the pictures out of his mind as he concentrated on putting his tools away. He took no further notice of the girls as they crossed the road and disappeared from sight.

TWO: A Dawn Ride

Stephanie sat on a low brick wall outside a garage, watching Poppy as the younger girl chattered away in the grimy-looking phone box. Poppy had announced her intention of making the call within minutes of their leaving the club and Stephanie, for the time being, was placing her fate in the little mischief's hands. Her shoulders ached slightly from the beating she had given her, and she wriggled them, trying to loosen the muscles, dropping her head forward so her long red hair screened her face. She was tired, she supposed, but her system was still racing with adrenaline. The minute they were on the move again, she knew she'd feel just fine.

Having finished her call, Poppy came clattering back across the concrete, tucking down her short skirt and licking her lips, an indefinable air of naughtiness enveloping her. Stephanie's spanking arm began to tingle again, only this time with wanting, but she forced the feeling away.

"Well?" she enquired as the younger girl reached her.

Poppy took her arm and pulled her to her feet. "Come on - we have to get to the tube station."

While she allowed herself to be made to walk, Stephanie had to protest at the destination. "Poppy, it's not even five o'clock, there won't be any tubes for hours!"

"I know that," Poppy giggled. "It's just that's the best place I could think of to meet up. Come on, it isn't far - at least, I don't think it is." She burrowed in her enormous

23

bag, pulled out a street map and consulted it for a moment, her tongue appearing briefly at the corner of her mouth, then set off, towing Stephanie along.

Poppy kept up a fast pace, though her feet were beginning to ache a little. However, the warm, throbbing pain in her bottom was a pleasant distraction, as were the possibilities that awaited her now that she had at least a temporary freedom. Budgie the biker would co-operate with her, she had no fears on that score, and who knew what kind of delightful toys Stephanie's flat might contain? Poppy had often felt she was born under a lucky star, and things like this stroke of fortune only confirmed her belief. Much as she enjoyed Budgie's company, she was fairly sure that Max would look for her there before long, and if she wasn't there, well, Max would never find her until she was good and ready to be found.

Stephanie was matching her speed, swinging her hips slightly as she walked, and Poppy wondered if she was as excited and eager for their adventures to begin as she herself was. The streets were almost entirely deserted, in that curious lull that comes when the last nightclubbers have made their way home, and the first early workers are still gulping their coffee. The moon was a quarter full, but cast enough light for them not to feel particularly nervous.

Max must be missing her by now. She'd chosen her night quite carefully, a night when Max was attending one of the lengthy formal business dinners that bored her to death, so he wouldn't be suspicious when she pleaded a headache and plans to go straight to bed, as she had done before - and paid for such 'laziness' in the Punishment Room the next day. He would be home by now, though, would have been home for two or three hours. Would he have remembered their conversation earlier in the week, or had he dismissed it the moment they left the room?

Poppy rather thought it would re-occur to him when he found her gone. The corners of her mouth curved in a wicked smile as she imagined her normally controlled husband running through the house, shouting her name, searching in every corner, before realising that she'd been as good as her word, and run away. Would he be asleep now? She could almost picture him, fast asleep in the big double bed, one hand on his immaculate cock, turning over in the night and waking up miserably as he felt the lack of a warm squirmy red-headed witchling beside him. It would do him no harm at all to realise that she meant what she said, that she wasn't to be taken for granted.

"Is there anyone likely to worry about you?" she asked Stephanie, who had fallen very silent.

Stephanie shook her head, then sighed. "Well, not really. There's an answerphone - leave it on all the time, but if you hear either Paul or Alex, and if they sound bothered, you could let them know I'm all right. In fact, maybe you could ring them anyway - the numbers are by the phone."

"I will, if you want," Poppy offered, quietly crossing her fingers behind her back. Whoever Paul and Alex were, they were no concern of hers. She looked up at the sky again, noting the paling of the purple clouds, the pinkish-grey glow towards the east. Dawn was on the way, the dawn of a new day, and a brand new adventure.

The tube station Poppy had picked for their rendezvous with her mystery friend was reached down a short turning off the main road, and fronted with a large car park that was bordered on one side by a warehouse, and on the other by a small grassy knoll and a substantial clump of trees - less of a brave attempt at landscaping than a bit of former wild woodland, presumably left there as some kind of concession to preserving rural London, Stephanie thought. There was one car in the car park, but as its windscreen was cracked in three places, and its back numberplate was missing, she assumed its original owner was unlikely to return for it within the next half hour. Both of them were pacing aimlessly round the car park, not talking. Steph's rubber jeans creaked slightly, and she noticed that Poppy was looking at them with a thoughtful expression.

"Something on your mind?" she asked. Poppy put one finger to the corner of her mouth, in a gesture that was clearly conscious and practised, but which remained sexy purely because it was deliberate.

"I was just thinking about clothes," she said, and waited. Stephanie, implacable, waited too, and Poppy sighed. "I just thought, you know, just in case anyone saw us leave - maybe we should swap."

Stephanie flicked her tongue against her teeth, considering for a moment. Hell, it made as much sense as anything else this lunatic night. She was letting the little bitch have her house - why not her clothes?

"OK - but what size are your feet? Mine are a seven."

"Five," Poppy owned, reluctantly. "But I don't suppose anyone will look at our shoes." She gripped the hem of her flirty blue dress, obviously intending to whip it off there and then. Steph shook her head, grinning in spite of herself.

"You really are a little trollop, stripping off in bloody car parks. Let's at least get into that doorway over there before you start flashing your minge at the world again." As she uttered this final sentence, a slight shiver went through her as she understood its import. Poppy wore no panties under that dress and she, Stephanie, wore none under her tight rubber jeans. Very soon she would be the one whose sex was on display to the whole wide world.

Now what was that going to feel like?

The large, darkened window of the station's newspaper kiosk was moderately useful as a mirror, and Stephanie found their joint reflection fascinating. Next to her, Poppy was standing with her shoulders back and chin out, thrusting her breasts forward in Stephanie's lacy black top, with Stephanie's red denim jacket slung round her shoulders. Steph herself now carried Poppy's white shoulder bag, from which the other had abstracted only her purse and own front door key. Poppy's blue dress clung even more tightly on Stephanie, and the early dawn air felt shockingly cool on her bare vulva, as well as stiffening her nipples, making them jut determinedly forward against the tight glossy fabric.

The roar of a motorbike engine, interrupting her musings, made her jump and swing round, reacting rather more girlishly than she would normally have done.

"Don't worry, it's all right, it's Budgie," Poppy said as the bike drew to a halt in the car park and the rider disembarked, fiddling with the strap of his crash helmet. She took Stephanie's hand in hers and led the way forward to where the biker waited with an unlit cigarette in his mouth, leaning against his machine.

With slowly reawakening lechery, Stephanie had been anticipating the oily, bearded, long-haired stereotype. But what confronted her now - wide hazel eyes glancing, then staring at the length of leg the borrowed blue dress revealed - was a stocky skinhead clad in black leather, with an open, humorous face, a huge silver ring in one ear, and a wicked grin.

"Brought a mate along then, Pops," he observed.

Poppy, who had originally looked about to rush up and hug the new arrival, stopped in her tracks and pouted.

"Well -" she began. "Well, she's not exactly - I mean,

didn't you listen? The plan is -"

Budgie raised his eyebrows. "If both of you want to come away, you silly cow, you should've said. Can't fit you both on the bike, can I?"

Poppy stamped her foot as Budgie, quite unconcerned, lit his cigarette. It was obvious to Stephanie that he was playing dumb and unco-operative on purpose, probably for the amusement value of winding Poppy up. The younger girl was twisting her hands together and bowing her head as she tried to convince him that he had already agreed in principle to taking Stephanie somewhere that she referred to as 'your lot'.

Stephanie wrapped her arms around herself, feeling the morning chill, the dawn of sobriety, and in a moment of clarity almost opened her mouth to call the whole scheme off - or at least, to put a stop to any further participation of her own. Poppy, however, already looked likely to start crying again, and Stephanie quietly challenged herself not to be such a bore. She'd just been handed a real-life adventure on a plate, and she'd surely regret it if she walked away. Who needed to be one hundred per cent safe all the time?

Poppy was still jabbering away at the biker when he suddenly reached out and clamped one hand firmly over her mouth.

"All right, that's enough. Christ on a side-car, you could talk for Britain, you could." He gave her head a rough shake, as though she were an obstinate dog, and let her go.

"All right," he said again. "I'll take your mate with me. But I think you owe me a little something for all this aggravation, Pops."

Poppy clasped her hands behind her back and swayed from foot to foot, acting up the girly-girl role she had chosen.

"Really, Budgie? What are you going to want?"

"Yeah, what do you want?" Steph enquired, moving up close behind Poppy and taking a good long, speculative look at the noticeable swelling in the front of Budgie's heavy leather jeans. Aware of her gaze, he looked her up and down in turn, running his tongue briefly over his lips as he took in how much of her shapely body was on display in Poppy's skimpy little dress.

"That little clump of trees," he nodded. "I think we'll take a walk over there, and I think I'll have five or ten minutes with that lovely arse of yours, Pops." His eyes flickered between the two girls, and he added to Stephanie, "I think I can find something to do with you, and all."

No further words were spoken as they left the bike where it was parked and crossed the wide crescent of the station approach to the grassy bank and the trees which shielded the station and the track from the nearby houses. There were not very many trees, but they were close together, and one of them, a weeping willow, was close enough to its rather stunted neighbour to provide something like the traditional rustic bower. From one of the other trees, Stephanie could hear a bird chirping, and she smiled to herself as the

three of them stood in the quiet greenness, in that curious moment of almost ritual silence that can occur when sex forms part of a bargain struck for better - or worse.

"Get those pants off, then, Pops," Budgie said, hooking his thumbs into the waistband of his leather jeans. Poppy stumbled a little as she extricated herself from her own clothes, stripping quite naked again before striking a pose, both hands on her hips and one leg slightly forward, revealing the dampness of her pubic hair, the faint glisten as her lubrication began to flow. She turned slowly, rotating like a ballerina-doll in a jewellery box, and

29

Budgie gave a soft whistle of appreciation at the sight of her bottom, still criss-crossed with red and pink and purple, a delicate but definite marbling of the soft, tender flesh.

"How do you want me?" Poppy asked, her voice a husky drawl. Steph could feel her own excitement building, wetness bubbling between her thighs, and she licked her lips as Budgie took hold of Poppy's breasts and began to knead them, roughly but not clumsily, squeezing the nipples so that they popped up hard, tight little acorns, dark against the girl's pale skin.

"Get on your knees," Budgie whispered. "On your knees with your arse in the air. And you -" he said to Stephanie, "come over here and strip me, slave girl. Get me ready."

It was as though her hands and body were not her own any more, as though she had taken on something of Poppy's self-hood when she had taken on the flimsy dress, because even as she was about to point out that she was the one who usually called the shots, she was moving right up close behind him, wrapping her arms around him, unfastening his leather jeans, and easing them slowly down over his hips.

"Boots," he said, and she froze, not understanding. "Get my boots off first, you silly cow."

He remained rigidly still as she crouched at his feet, fumbling with the buckled straps that fastened his heavy bike boots. The smell of leather filled her head, the deep, sweet smell that always sent faint, lustful tremors through the whole of her body. The only move he made to help her was to lift each foot in turn, allowing her to slide off boot and sock and finally to pull the heavy leather jeans the rest of the way down his legs and remove them altogether. His arms were folded and his eyes had taken on a dreamy, heavy-lidded look, as though he were drifting away into a world of limitless sexual explorations. His cock, which was stubby but thick, pushed proudly forward, darkening with arousal and gleaming faintly as the foreskin retracted to reveal the sticky head, smothered with the earliest droplets of thin, clear fluid. On her knees, with her marked bottom high in the air, Poppy was wanking herself, balancing on one hand while the other juddered and fretted between her legs.

Budgie finally moved his hands, patting the breast pockets of his leather jacket and unzipping one to extract a tube of lubricant, which he held out to Stephanie.

"Get her ready for it," he said.

As Stephanie took the lube from him, he took hold of himself, one hand working his shaft, the other fondling his balls, lifting and moving them in their soft, slack bag of skin. Stephanie found herself glancing to and fro, between his leisurely hand movements and Poppy's quivering buttocks. She uncapped the lubricant, wondering as she did so what special properties it possessed that could not already be served by Poppy's copious natural production. Perhaps it made the skin tingle, or smelt good, she thought, half-amused, and squeezed a little over her fingers, gently nudging Poppy's own fingers aside to smear the clear, sloppy gel over her swollen vaginal lips.

"Not there." The voice made her jump, and she realised that Budgie was now crouching beside her, his breath hot on her cheek.

"Not her cunt. She's sloppy enough already. Put it up her arse. Open up her back door for me."

Stephanie was not, herself, particularly accustomed to anal sex, but now she understood the need for lubricant. She wondered what Poppy thought of the idea, but a glance at her excited face, indicating that Poppy had heard and understood, stopped her from interrupting or disagreeing with Budgie about what he clearly intended to do. She squirted another big glob of lubricating gel into her hand, relishing its slippery coolness, and slapped the whole handful against the crack of Poppy's bottom, trailing her fingers through it and smearing it all around the younger girl's arsehole. Poppy, still diddling her clit, whimpered appreciatively as Steph ran her finger around and around the crinkled opening, pushing against it for entry, teasing the delicate skin.

"That's enough," Budgie said, grabbing her wrist and moving her hand out of the way. "You take care of your own pussy, and I'll take care of her."

Steph almost overbalanced as he pushed her aside, but found she didn't mind too much as he took up his position behind the kneeling, trembling girl. He started by using his thumbs on Poppy, pushing her buttocks apart and easing first one, then both thumbs into the now thoroughly lubricated hole. His cock seemed to nod in approval as he withdrew his hands, smiling, and shuffled forward. Poppy began to purr as he gripped her hips and steadily eased himself inside her. Steph, lying back on the soft, damp grass, realised that she, too, was thoroughly damp, her pussy walls engorged and swollen. The skirt of the little dress was rucked up, and she made a move to tug it down to a less revealing level, but Budgie had been keeping an eye on her.

"Go on, wank yourself - you must be dying to," he ordered, never stopping his steady in-and-out movements. "And I want to see you come."

Steph hesitated, then it occurred to her that so far in the night's excitements she hadn't had an orgasm of her own, and her pussy was almost hurting now with the need for satisfaction. She spread her legs wider apart to allow her greedy fingers access to her quim. She was even wetter than she had thought, and her fingers slipped in easily as she began to frig herself in real earnest. Poppy and Budgie

were screwing in near silence, the girl using both arms for balance now as Budgie mauled her breasts with one hand and attacked her clit with the other. Stephanie began to rub her own clitoris harder and faster,
a warm trembling building in the pit of her stomach as her climactic convulsions drew closer. Then the wave was upon her and she gasped, scissoring her legs as she thrust the heel of her hand hard against her quim. Poppy was squealing now, little sharp cries, obviously coming too, and finally Steph saw Budgie squeeze his eyes shut, his buttocks jerked two or three times, and he pulled out of Poppy with a sigh, discharging one final squirt of semen onto the grass.

There was a moment's pause, then Budgie wiped his face with his forearm.

"Not a bad bargain, girls, not bad at all," he observed. He picked up his leather jeans, and began to dress. Poppy did the same, and Stephanie watched the two of them, thinking that there were certain advantages to the borrowed minidress - like not having to struggle in and out of clothes every time a girl felt in the mood.

No more was said until they were back by the bike, when Stephanie put her arms round Poppy and hugged her.

"Good luck - and don't forget to tell my boys where I am," she said, with a quick pinch of the other's hot, damp buttock.

Poppy kissed her full on the mouth. "Don't worry, everything's going to be fine," she said. "I'll come and get you when it's all sorted out. Thanks for doing this, Steph - I mean it."

One final mutual squeeze, one quick kiss for Budgie, and then she turned and began to walk back towards the main road, presumably heading for the minicab office they had passed on the way to the station.

"Well ..." Steph murmured, suddenly feeling chilly. She opened Poppy's bag and rummaged inside, wondering if there might be anything by way of additional clothes in there. Budgie grinned as she finally extracted a see-through black chiffon blouse, of the type clearly designed to tie under the breasts rather than tuck into a skirt. She put it on anyway, and he unstrapped two crash helmets from the bike and handed her one.

"Sling your leg over, slave girl, and let's get out of here." His tone was friendly rather than instructional, but Steph found herself on the verge of pointing out that she really wasn't accustomed to being told what to do. Still, she swallowed the words and, helmet buckled tightly into position, climbed aboard the bike. With vague memories of lifts home from pubs in her late teens, she looked for the leather strap that should be across the saddle between herself and the rider, but found none. Budgie turned his head, somehow more sinister with his face hidden behind a curved screen of smoky glass.

"Ain't no strap. Hold on round my waist." He didn't wait for her either to reply or obey, but revved the bike's engine with a thunderous roar, and it was only with the purest effort of will that Stephanie stopped herself from clamping her arms around him like a panicky octopus.

Still, she reflected as the two-wheeled monster spun round in a wide circle and hurled itself at the empty road, no one could say the end of the night had been boring.

There was still very little traffic on the roads as they sped through unfamiliar suburbs, though the sky was slowly turning a paler, pearlier grey and the temperature starting to rise. With her hands resting loosely on Budgie's hips and her head against his back, Stephanie found herself smiling widely with a rush of exhilaration. The big bike was fast, but smooth, and Budgie handled it with absolute, instinctive confidence. Freed from any fear of falling, of a sudden messy end in the middle of nowhere, Stephanie gave herself over to absolute sensation. The steady thrumming of the engine transmitted itself in a low, buzzing vibration through the seat, made more intense because of her lack of panties. She tensed her thighs, leaning with the movement as they roared round a bend, then wriggled her bottom to intensify the pleasant stimulation. The little blue dress was blowing up almost to her waist, and she knew that her bare buttocks could be seen by anyone they passed.

Steph knew she had a lovely bottom; Alex, Paul and several of her past partners had complimented her on its sweet, peachy curves. However, this was the first time she had put it so much on display; made that part of herself so freely available to the careless or lustful gaze of anyone who happened along. So far, admittedly, they had passed very few vehicles, and the bike was travelling at enough of a speed for no more than the merest could-I-be-dreaming glimpse of her naked rear to be seen, but somehow she almost wanted more traffic - wanted to be noticed.

She had been used to regard any view of her bottom or breasts as a privilege that had to be earned by her playmates, a goal for them to work towards, but now this prize was free, attainable to anyone, any chance encounter. Her pussy began to pulse again and, nose and mouth brushing the oily leather of Budgie's jacket, she smiled.

The last of the suburbs were dwindling away when Budgie turned off the motorway and headed down a leafy, tree-lined B-road. Now the sun was fully risen, a warm, golden light slowly bathing the landscape, glinting off the surface of a wide canal that flowed under the motorway bridge, brightening the intense but somehow blowsy, peaking greens of grass and trees. They turned left at a roundabout, right at the next one, then right again down a much narrower road, marked only with a white-painted wooden signpost. Now Budgie reduced his speed, and Stephanie sat back with a little sigh. The deep, glorious vibrations had dwindled, and the amazing glow in her pussy was diminishing with them.

After several more twists and turns in the road, they came to a low wooden fence, edging an expanse of long, golden green grass, merging into trees that grew like a screen of some kind between the road and whatever lay beyond.

Budgie slowed the bike even more as they reached a gap in the fence, with a sign on a long metal pole. Stephanie gave a little gasp as she saw the painting so blatantly displayed. While rather crudely done, there was no mistaking the image, nor its implications: a bold outline of a girl, bending over to display a bottom barely covered by brief shorts, clutching her buttocks with one hand and holding the other to her mouth in exaggerated shock and surprise. If there had been any doubt in Stephanie's mind it was utterly dispelled by the word underneath the drawing - one word in sprawling capitals: TANNERS.

Nothing was said as Budgie steered the bike along the dusty road through the trees to the brink of a gentle downward slope, where it crossed what appeared to be a circular, stony path, more of a track than a road. He pulled up for a moment, parking at an angle that gave Stephanie her first glimpse of a collection of buildings, all timbered, with corrugated iron roofs, some large, others smaller, arranged in a semi-circle around a kind of rough courtyard where a dozen or so bikes and one large van were parked. Woods seemed to surround the settlement, enclosing it like possessive arms on three sides, but the feeling she got from the place was one of security rather than confinement. It looked as though it were hidden away to keep the curious or hostile out, rather than to keep the reluctant visitor in, and she found herself eager to see it more closely.

She was about to get off the bike, about to speak, when Budgie gunned the engine into life and peeled off abruptly to the left. The dirt road veered outwards, curving around, plunging back into the trees, presumably circling the buildings entirely, but Budgie halted again at a point where it broadened out into a small clearing, with dense woods on one side and a thinning out of the trees on the other. This time he switched the engine off completely and unbuttoned his crash helmet. Slinging the helmet over the handlebar, he turned round in the saddle. "Take yours off then."

Shrugging, Stephanie did so, before disembarking. He took the helmet from her, grasped her by her other wrist and pulled her close enough to kiss her firmly, pushing her lips apart with his tongue. Steph responded willingly, even though she had not expected the move. He was gripping her upper arms quite firmly, and did not let go when he moved his mouth from hers.

"All right, slave girl, few things to settle," he said with a smirk. He clearly had more to say, but Steph momentarily forgot herself.

"My name is Stephanie, not slave," she said petulantly, then stopped, alarmed. He didn't seem annoyed, but his crooked smile widened.

"Definitely a few things to settle then, Stephanie," he remarked quietly. "Time we got it sorted out, I reckon."

Steph waited, no longer worried. At least, not exactly. He seemed to be waiting in turn, for her to say something else, but she felt inclined to keep silent.

"Thing is, girl, I've spent a lot of time with Poppy before. She knows the score, but I don't think you do - yet."

Stephanie licked her lips, beginning to feel uneasy again, but trying to reassure herself. Budgie had seemed relatively trustworthy so far, and she had always prided herself on her sound instincts.

He was still smiling, and something about his general demeanour made the pulse between her legs, still tingling from the earlier stimulation of the fast bike ride, increase its intensity.

"We look after our girls here, slave girl," Budgie explained. "So long as they do as they're told, we treat 'em just right. But we have to keep them in hand. Do you get my meaning?"

Stephanie was fairly sure she did, but decided to pretend that she didn't. She shook her head and, rather to her own surprise, widened her eyes and crossed one foot over the other in a manner very reminiscent of Poppy's earlier behaviour. Budgie stopped talking for a moment to give her a thoroughly appreciative grin.

"Not bad," he observed. He reached out and squeezed her breasts, not cruelly, but not gently, either. Steph didn't flinch, and he nodded to himself.

"You'll do. Oh, you'll do. We won't say anything to the rest about Poppy, just that you're my new little slave girl."

Again she considered asking him not to call her that, but decided it wouldn't be prudent. She put her hands behind her back, and waited for his next move.

"Little slave girl," Budgie mused. "Some girls ain't so little though, and some need it more than others." His dark eyes met hers again. "And some bikers talk bollocks - isn't that what you're thinking?"

Stephanie almost said yes, then shook her head.

"Bad girl. Disrespectful girl, talking back. That'll do. Come on then, bend over, bend over the bike, that's it, lovely. Get that arse up in the air. I reckon it needs a good bit of warming up after all that riding around, waving it in the breeze, don't you?"

Stephanie knew that a refusal to comply might well terminate her adventures there and then, and though she told herself she was obeying out of a wish to see how far things would actually go, her decision to position herself thus, head and hands resting on the still-warm padded leather of the seat, bottom raised, carried with it a powerful anticipatory charge, a taut excitement that seemed to transmit and retransmit in a fast circuit between her nipples and her clit.

Budgie took the hem of her skirt in both hands and began to fold it upwards with a precise, almost ritualistic series of turns. Once her bottom was utterly bared to the morning air, he spent two or three minutes just caressing it, running his slightly roughened hands over the soft skin again and again. Steph's nostrils were filled with a heavy, exciting scent, a mixture of warm leather and her own arousal, her own fragrance transmitted to the seat during the journey. Budgie's hands on her bum had grown more insistent, rubbing and squeezing the flesh of her cheeks, and suddenly he lifted his palm and brought it down again in a swift slap. Stephanie jumped slightly, more from surprise than pain, but before she had time to think that this wasn't so bad, that it was really nothing, three or four light slaps had been followed by three slightly harder ones, and one, landing squarely across the crack of her arse, that made her gasp aloud. Clearly presuming her to be well warmed up by now, Budgie began to spank her thoroughly, rhythmically, steadily, distributing the smacks evenly all over her bottom. She dug her nails into the leather, gritting her teeth, determined to bear it, determined not to let it get to her. She thought briefly of Paul, who she had often spanked, remembering what he said about the thrill of it, the glow that spreads steadily through you, turning on all your nerve endings at once.

She flexed and tensed her thigh muscles and her belly as the spanking continued, and found herself beginning to understand what Paul had meant. The warm throbbing in her buttocks was steadily transmitting itself to her vulva, which was beginning to ache with that sweet, sweet ache, feeling swollen and heavy, the inner walls weeping, slick with fluid. Sh breathed in the leathery musk from the seat and moved her face against it, almost kittenishly.

"Oh, you're ready now, all right," she heard Budgie say, and the rain of blows came to an end. She would have protested, but the hand that had spanked her was now questing between her thighs. He found her clitoris, and rubbed it hard, gripping her around the waist with his other hand and holding her steady as she orgasmed violently, squealing, hips jerking, juices gushing from her quim.

When it was over, and she was able to lift her head, she saw Budgie looking at her with a mixture of satisfaction and superiority that seemed to characterise a dominant's feelings for any little slut who could come so intensely from being punished. As she stood up, she noticed the erection distending his jeans. Taking in the direction of her gaze, he cupped his hand over it and rubbed himself through the tight leather.

"You as good with your hands as I am with mine?" he asked. He unzipped himself, tugging the jeans down only far enough to allow the egress of his prick, now fully erect, the glans gleaming with his secretions.

Stephanie took a step forward, pressing herself up close against him as she grasped him firmly, running her thumb over the tip of his cock as she slid her fingers up and down the shaft. His hands closed on her breasts and he pinched and tugged her nipples through her dress as she continued to wank him, varying the pace between light, gliding upward and downward strokes, and a tighter grip combined with faster movements.

His hips thrust forward, and he began to pant hard. Stephanie moved her hand even faster, bringing her other one into play to stroke his testicles and reach behind them to that sweetly sensitive few centimetres of skin. Budgie moaned, throwing his head back, and pulled her hard against him when she would have turned aside, his hands suddenly on her shoulders, pushing her downwards onto her knees so that the jets of spunk went over her breasts, streaking and splashing the blouse and dress, a few drops landing in her hair, a few on her face.

When Budgie's bike finally pulled up in the centre of the courtyard, some minutes later, Stephanie contemplated the fact that this was probably the least conventional entrance she had ever made - hair a tangled mess, bottom glowing and smarting not unpleasantly from her first real spanking, and semen all over her clothes. And this, she told herself brightly, was only the beginning.

THREE: More Than This

At a quarter past midnight, six days after Poppy and Stephanie had met each other, Club Sevrina was packed and jumping. Subs, doms, masters, mistresses, slaves and playmates milled happily around, meeting, mingling, exchanging kisses, spanks and gossip, all set on having a damn good time. Sevrina's regular venue, a night-club normally known as the Top Hat, was divided into two floors, a dance floor with a bar at one end, and a quieter, darker upper room where the stocks, the cages, the whipping stools and crosses were set up each month, and where a variety of wanton, wicked and wonderful games were played.

Paul Henwood, who had decided on the spur of the moment that there was nothing to stop him going out alone, had spent an hour or so hoping to bump into Stephanie, but had not been successful. It had irked him at first, but striving to ignore it had made him almost unconsciously hold up his head and straighten his shoulders, and he was interested to realise that he had begun to feel unusually in control. He had told himself firmly to stop thinking about Stephanie, and concentrate on enjoying whatever other pleasures a night of absolute liberation might have to offer. Pleasures indeed were promised to him now, and he was dimly aware at the back of his mind that he had attracted quite an audience, but it only added to his sense of satisfaction.

He struck a pose for a moment, relishing the picture he

must make, his fair hair slicked back, his beard neatly trimmed, vaguely menacing in his tight black jodhpurs and white shirt. With one hand in his pocket, he drew the other back slowly, extending as far as possible the arm that held the cat of soft red leather, the one Stephanie had left in his flat the previous week, the one he was about to bring down across the shoulders of the petite, pretty blonde he had just finished cuffing to the bronze-painted wooden St Andrew's cross by the stairs.

Lydia, that was her name, and she had made the first move, whether or not she had actually believed the dominant persona he was currently cultivating. Had she sought him out as some kind of challenge to him, rather than to herself, seeing the usually submissive soul behind the haughty mask? Had she expected him to stumble, falter, turn her down? She would believe in his mastery now, and so would he. There was no sense of boundary-crossing, no sense of wrongdoing - just a fascination, a thrill, a delight in experiment.

He shifted his balance from left to right foot and swung the cat, which described a lovely arc through the air and made a lusty smacking sound as it connected. OK, shift the balance back, pivot from the hips and bring it down again to cross the first set of marks - he could almost hear the voice in his head. He did it again, and then again, and stepped back slightly, drawing the tails of the whip through his other hand before aiming the next strokes at Lydia's trembling bottom. It took a certain amount of concentration to perform with aplomb, but he was beginning to appreciate the advantages of being on this end of the whip. He whirled the cat around his head, around again and down, enjoying the little squeal this provoked from the blonde, who was beginning to writhe enticingly against the cross. She wore nothing but three triangles of white leather, linked by silver chains to form a g-string and minimal bra. Her feet were clad in high-heeled scarlet patent shoes with heavy silver buckles, matching the scarlet leather wristcuffs and collar she wore as a visible, flaunting mark of her particular preference.

As he trailed the whip gently down her spine she twisted in her bonds, letting him see that the pale pink nipples of her cute little breasts had stiffened perceptibly. Moving right up close, he bent his head and bit the left one, nipping gently at the tautly swollen bud and making her sigh with delight. As he stepped back to prepare his aim for the second bout of whipping, he felt a touch on his arm and a tall, slender Asian girl offered him a customised riding crop, the end of which had been replaced by a triangular piece of scarlet leather.

"She like this. I see her take it lots of times," the girl advised. Paul raised his eyebrows, feeling his already-rising cock give another twinge of excitement, and took the proffered implement, tucking Stephanie's cat into one of his boots.

The little blonde's low, purring moan as the first swipe landed on her left buttock proved the truth of the assertion, and Paul began to beat her steadily, keeping time with the rhythm of the music pounding through the playroom – *I wanna Be Your Dog*, with that raw driving bass and the lyrical intimation of sleazy surrender. He was breaking out in a light sweat, as much from arousal as from exertion, and now he understood what Stephanie had meant the time she told him about the near-trance state it was possible to reach when applying a whip, cane or tawse to a willing backside. Much as he appreciated the slender, shapely blonde in front of him, the pretty little creature whose bottom was now turning a deep blushing red, he still couldn't help allowing Stephanie into his thoughts now and again; mental flashes of Steph herself chained and submissive before him, begging him to beat her, slap her, and take her passionately fast, deliriously rough. He wondered briefly if his red-headed bitch goddess had ever harboured any trace of a masochistic fantasy, then reapplied himself to the job in hand. Stephanie was incommunicado at present, and he was far too pleasurably occupied right now to care.

Lydia was heaving in her bonds now, moaning like a queen cat on heat, and he stopped beating her to see if she was as turned-on as her behaviour would suggest. She parted her legs eagerly as he thrust his hand between them, and he thought she might have begged for something, but he chose not to listen. His fingers touched oily, oozy wetness and folds of hot, swollen flesh, making him wonder whether or not to rub her to orgasm. A more audacious idea took possession of him, and he handed the crop back to its owner before freeing Lydia's feet and then her hands.

"Here," he said, laconically, towing her through the crowd by means of the ring attached to her red leather collar. Against a nearby wall was a low, wide bench topped with black rubber, and he draped himself over it, unzipping his jodhpurs with one hand and pulling her head down with the other.

"Get to work, bitch," he growled as he wrapped his fingers round his shaft. She crouched, evidently ready to suck him, but he slapped her lightly on the cheek.

"Not like that. Sit over my face so I can see how much you like it. Then you can suck me off."

She clearly thought he was going to oblige her in the same way, wiggling her sodden cleft over his nose and mouth, showing him just how excited she was, drops of moisture clinging to the fine chains of her leather g-string. When Paul didn't lick at her pussy she paused in her eager but slightly clumsy oral attentions to his cock, which was hard almost to bursting point.

Reaching up, he smacked her already bruised bottom, and she began again, taking him further into her warm, soft mouth, and swirling her tongue around his rigid length. Enjoying the sensations immensely, he relaxed a little, watching with some interest the way her vaginal muscles were clenching and unclenching in frantic desperation. The leather cat was still in his boot, tails curled round the shaft, and he brought it out, reversing it so that the leather-wrapped handle was uppermost. Slowly, he began to tease Lydia's clit with the very end of the whip, rubbing the slightly roughened seam directly against the pebble-hard, sweating bead of flesh. With her fingers working the base of his cock, she raised her head for a moment to wail her pleasure, and he pushed the stock of the cat right inside her, twisting it gently to stretch her inner walls further, and force her to a swaying, sobbing climax. Moaning and dribbling, she kissed his cock again, poking her tongue into the tiny opening, and Paul began to come, shuddering as the hot jets escaped, grinding his teeth in the final spasms to keep back the name that flashed across his mind, the name it would be vastly impolite to cry out right now – *Stephanie*!

Alex McCoy pulled his elderly Granada up outside the dark façade of the Top Hat and switched the engine off as he scanned the stragglers moving away from the building. Dark-haired, dark-eyed, with a known preference for dressing mainly in black, Alex liked to consider himself a creature of the night. Driving a mini-cab and sleeping all day was a lifestyle that suited him, providing as it did plenty of opportunities to meet women, many of whom, disappointed in their night's misses on the dance floors and in the bars, were more than keen to embark on flirtations and even fornications with a sympathetic, sleazily good-looking mini-cab man. Many a journey was interrupted by some detour to the park gates, a dark alley or some nearly-deserted car park for a fiddle, a suck or a fuck in the back seat, over the bonnet or, at this time of year, in the long grass or quickly consummated on his old leather jacket flung down on gravel or concrete.

His fare this time was a girl called Lydia, who, according to Control, was a blonde wearing a pale blue raincoat. Not that she needed a raincoat in this weather, but Alex knew all about the Top Hat and guessed that she probably had next to nothing on underneath it – a tempting prospect, with a bit of luck. He saw her then, heading towards him and, to Alex's disappointment, leading a broad-shouldered, fair-haired man along with her. Scratch this one for any additional servicing, he thought as he leaned back to open the car door. Restarting the engine, he waited for them to climb inside.

"Where to, mate?"

"Drover Road, please, the fire station end."

Now he heard it, he knew the bloke's voice. Well, well, well, Steph's little puppy-dog Paul was out on the rampage without her. Alex struggled to straighten his face, wondering if the other would recognise him in turn. He supposed his thoughts about Paul were less than charitable, really – it wasn't as if Stephanie had ever asked or expected either of them to stick to her and her alone. Glancing in the mirror, he could tell that Paul's eyes were on him, and he wasn't surprised when he spoke up.

"Alex, isn't it?"

"That's me. Seen anything of Steph lately?" Paul's brow creased, and Alex choked back a laugh. Oopsy – maybe that wasn't going to go down too well with the pretty little number in the blue coat. Mind you, she had her head on Paul's shoulder and looked like she was dropping off to sleep. Paul was playing with her hair, winding the curly golden strands around his fingers, and Alex was surprised by the edgy tone in his voice when he finally answered.

"No, not a thing all week. How about you?"

"Nothing. Must be working on another script, I guess." Or another bloke, Alex added to himself. Devoid of jealousy, he enjoyed screwing Stephanie on an occasional basis as it was a characteristic they shared. Well, that and her appetite for lusciously perverted sex, handcuffs and a whip or two, gags and blindfolds... Alex grinned as he remembered the last time she'd chained him to her bed and sucked him off with a mouthful of brandy. Personally, he didn't care for the heavy stuff, but a little bit of spice just made things go a bit better. He had picked up on the fact that she went in for some pretty outrageous antics with Paulie-Boy, but so what?

Paul's little blondie half woke up before either of the men could think of anything else to say to one another, and seemed in need of some attention. Hitching up her raincoat so the skirt of it flapped open, she spread her legs, revealing the very skimpy bit of leather and chain that served her for panties. She grabbed Paul's hand and put it decisively between her thighs, pushing at his fingers to make her meaning clear. Alex was very glad that the roads were clear of traffic, as he barely managed to keep his mind or eyes on the road ahead, given the dirty spectacle taking place in his back seat. Whatever Paul might be feeling about Stephanie's absence, Paul was certainly wanking off his new friend with a will. The steady sounds, a soughing and a sticky, lip-smacking noise were making Alex hard. Risking another glance in the mirror, his eyes met the reflection of Paul's, and there was a moment of curious complicity that had to do with more than the actuality of this present, pretty little blonde nympho. There was a link between the two of them - a currently missing but much-loved, demanding, delicious, red-headed connection, and both of them knew it.

Sunday afternoon was calm and still, sun beating steadily down from a clear blue sky, and the temperature heading inexorably for the record books. Though it clashed with his chosen persona, Alex actually had nothing against a sunny afternoon to spend as he chose. Right now, he was spending it in what should have been ideal circumstances; tucked behind a clump of trees in the Green Street cemetery, with a big straw beach mat, a bottle of red wine and the gorgeous, plump, lush-lipped and predatory Elaine Brown. She was currently lying on her belly, her head with its sleek brown bob pillowed on her crossed hands, her lightly tanned legs shown off by a tight, frayed denim miniskirt and her large breasts flaunted in an equally tight white t-shirt.

Alex, sitting with his back against an oblong stone tomb, sipped wine from the bottle and divided his glances between Elaine, admiring her bum and her soft chubby thighs, and a memorial stone angel a few feet away. Time and lichens had somehow altered what must once have been a pious expression into a faintly knowing one, and the angel's posture, arms outstretched and upturned, made Alex think of a slave lashed to a wall, awaiting the pleasure of a master or mistress, the caress of a lash against that slender back. He'd seen pictures of submissives like that in magazines, but he couldn't help raising an eyebrow at the turn his thoughts were taking. He crossed his legs and glanced back down at Elaine, who did not move.

He sighed. Elaine was a very sexy lady, but there were times when she could be a serious pain in the neck. All right, so he'd brought her here hoping to screw her, he'd never denied it, and the first couple of times he'd screwed her, once behind the garden shed during a party, the night they'd met, and once in his car, parked in a deserted multi-storey, she hadn't raised any objections. He had never promised her anything other than sex, and the sex had been good for her as well as for him, so why the sudden moody? All he'd done was mention the encounter of the previous night – meeting Stephanie's other boyfriend out with another girlfriend. He'd expected Elaine to see the funny side, but she had developed a serious attack of the sulks, and it looked like he was in for an entire afternoon of it.

He took another swallow of the wine and leaned forward, holding out the bottle.

"Sure you don't want some?" She rolled over onto her side, and took the wine from him, frowning. She drank several long gulps, and handed it back.

"So what's she like then, this Stephanie?" she demanded.

"She's a girl. A red-haired girl that I like to fuck," Alex said, pushing his hair out of his eyes. Elaine sat up, and he noticed that she wasn't frowning any more.

"That's not what I meant," she snapped, and Alex looked at her more closely. Her eyes were very bright, and she licked her lips with a slow sliding motion of her tongue that sent an immediate signal to Alex's groin.

"I meant, what does she like? What does she do? Does she bang in gangs?" Elaine drawled. "Does she go with other girls? If I have to share you with her, then I'll share - but I want to share *thoroughly*. Why don't you take me round to meet her?"

Alex nearly dropped the bottle of wine. "Yeah? When?"

"How about now?"

Whether Elaine's suggestion was motivated by lechery or by some kind of competitive impulse, she'd made it, and she seemed pretty set on the idea. It was definitely one that appealed to Alex. He took one more sip of the wine and pushed the cork back into the bottleneck. "OK, we'll go see if she's in. Take her the rest of this as a peace offering, I guess. Come on."

She was already on her feet, brushing a few bits of dried grass off her legs.

"Good," she said.

The entryphone system to Stephanie's flat hadn't worked in six months, so Alex led Elaine through the heavy glass door and straight up the stairs, the stairway shadowy cool and smelling faintly of floor polish, until they reached the second floor, and the cream-painted door. Alex knocked the usual knock - three-two-one - and waited for an answer. Elaine was shifting from foot to foot, as though her panties were chafing her vulva, a habit he had noticed before when she was sexually excited. She caught him looking at her and smirked. Alex, smirking in return, wondered if Steph was in bed with someone else, and how that would go down, so to speak. A frisky foursome might be on the agenda, but then again, so might the marching orders for Elaine and himself. He wondered momentarily how that would feel, if Stephanie actually dropped him cold. There was no answer, so he knocked again, the pattern, three-two-one, so Stephanie would know who it was.

Elaine sighed. "Maybe she's out."

"Maybe." Alex was disappointed. His hard-on had subsided slightly, though he thought it would probably come back with a little assistance from Elaine. Maybe he'd better take her back to her place, do her in her big bed, save the threesome idea for another day. Elaine, however, was pink-cheeked with excitement, revving herself up, clearly not at all inclined to give up this easily.

"Don't you have a key then, seeing as you're such *good friends*?" she taunted. "We could just pop inside and wait for her - give her a fuck-o-gram."

Alex considered for a moment then, rather against his better judgement, stretched up and ran his hand along the top of the doorframe. He remembered Steph saying she kept a spare key up there in case she locked herself out - he'd thought at the time that it was a pretty dumb idea for such a smart lady, but he wasn't sorry about it now. His fingers closed on the key and he brought it down to the lock with a little murmur of triumph. He had to admit that her week long silence had bothered him a bit - maybe he could find some sort of clue as to her whereabouts or intentions inside.

Stephanie's flat looked much as Stephanie's flat always did - cluttered but comfortable. Of the owner, there was no sign, but an open book on the kitchen table and a bottle of pink lemonade left open and out of the fridge suggested that she wasn't planning to be away for very long. Elaine announced that she needed to pee and, having pointed her in the direction of the bathroom, Alex wandered into the living room, looking at the familiar mess; shoes every-where, the long braided leather whip dropped on the seat of a chair, CDs out of their cases. Her green satin blouse was crumpled on the floor and he picked it up, detecting faint traces of the spicy perfume she usually wore.

"Alex ..."

He turned, almost guiltily, dropping the garment, and his attention was instantly distracted by the fact that Elaine had emerged from the bathroom stark naked, her rosy nipples jutting out in tight peaks, her lips moist, grinning at him.

"What the *fuck*?"

"I thought we could maybe start without her," Elaine said, spreading her legs and putting one hand on the damp curls of her pussy hair. "She's got a lovely big bed through there. Black satin sheets and everything. What do you reckon?"

Alex's head reckoned, in fact, that Elaine was pushing her luck a bit, but his cock reckoned that she looked devastatingly horny.

"Look, why don't we just go back to yours and ball?" he suggested, but Elaine shook her head.

"I don't want to wait, I want your prick in me now," she said. "I'm dripping with it, Alex, you've got to fuck me. Fuck me in her bed, she won't mind."

Alex wanted to argue some more, but his imagination was beginning to race ahead, to holding Elaine down and fucking her hard, biting those lovely boobs and feeling her wet, willing quim enclose him - and then what if Stephanie walked in on them? How would she react? What kind of pleasurable punishments would she mete out to the pair of them – to *him*, for his rudeness? And what, indeed, might she do to Elaine? Spank the cheeky little bitch, or whip her, or … His cock seemed to surge against his zip, and he took the two steps necessary to bring him across the room and within reach of Elaine, whose fingers had now begun to probe the folds of her quim. Alex pounced, grabbing her upper arms and sinking his teeth lightly but decidedly into the soft hollow beneath her collarbone. She squealed and shuddered against him, and he got one arm round her shoulders, snaked the other round her buttocks and whipped her off her feet, holding her tight against his chest as he carried her across the hall and into Stephanie's bedroom. He loved to pick a woman up and carry her off, knowing that it usually gave the woman a thrill, particularly as he was far stronger than his narrow-hipped body made him appear.

When he dropped Elaine onto the bed she spread her legs, showing him the wetness of the ripe pink quim beneath the fluffy veiling of dark hair. She was smiling widely, licking her lips, and Alex suddenly wanted her very much, wanted her more than enough for the thought of having her to drive all other considerations out of his head. Still dressed, he dropped onto the bed and began to kiss her navel, running his tongue over the curve of her belly, teasing the flesh of her inner thighs with his thumbs, kissing his way down until his bottom lip was just touching the very top of her wet opening. He paused then, just long enough for her to wriggle, thrust upwards with her hips and voice a little petulant whimper of frustrated lust.

Pulling her pussy lips apart, he ran his tongue from top to bottom in one moist, affectionate swipe, down and back up, down and back up, the juices bubbling and pooling in her quim as he reached upwards, reached her breasts and tweaked the already taut and quivering nipples, moved his hands back down again to hold her thighs while he ravaged her with his mouth, feeling her moving against him, hearing her wails and broken phrases of passion, holding her down, holding her steady, taking extra pleasure from his own detachment, his own restraint. She came against his face, squealing, thighs scissoring upwards and he let go, let her go with it, propping himself up on one hand and tearing at his clothes with the other. One swift movement pulled the t-shirt over his head, but when he unfastened his flies she still hadn't enough control over her limbs to offer assistance. He leaned over to kiss her tummy again as he tugged his jeans and pants down, dragging them off together with his old deck shoes, making himself as naked as the girl who still writhed beneath him.

Her breathing was slowing a little as he felt her quim, pushing a finger in and setting her off again, seeing her squirm and mutter to herself. He pushed a little harder, flicking her swollen clit, and her thighs strained apart, tense with wanting, and she looked up at him, panting slightly.

"You're ready to be fucked," he remarked, almost conversationally, and plunged himself inside her. She was slick and dripping, and her pussy closed around him like a velvet vice, gripping him passionately as he thrust into her harder and harder, grabbing her clutching hands and holding them firmly above her head, biting her neck and upper chest, licking the sweat from her throat, kissing her mouth and eyes, fucking her for all he was worth.

The black satin sheets of the tumbled bed were slippery-cool against his knees, and the contrast between them and Elaine's hot, sweaty-oily body against his was glorious, spectacular, and he moaned, nibbling her neck as he felt his balls tighten and draw up. Elaine was coming again, thrashing violently in his arms and he drew in a half-strangled breath, held her even tighter and came, groaning with pleasure, thinking and feeling nothing but the moment itself, the marvellous shuddering rush of completion.

They rolled over, laughing now, laughing with the happy exhilaration that often follows orgasm. Elaine's eyelashes were damp, starry, her lips swollen in the aftermath of the greedy kisses she'd snatched in the final seconds.

The black curtains in the bedroom were almost closed, but stayed apart sufficiently to allow a shaft of golden August light to penetrate the room. Stephanie's bedroom, even messier than usual, smelling faintly of lilac incense, and of Stephanie's Giorgio perfume, and of sexual repletion, the latter smell overwhelming the others. Alex closed his eyes for a moment, then opened them abruptly as Elaine tweaked his nose. "Hey!"

"Hey, there." He kissed her, because she clearly expected him to, but his mind was beginning to wander. There was probably no harm done, but maybe it had been a little bit ... ill-mannered, to do another girl in

Stephanie's bed. Then again, he thought, with a flash of petulance that surprised him, it wasn't like Steph to leave it this long without a word to him of her whereabouts or inclinations.

"I thought the idea was to wait for your friend Stephanie," Elaine observed. She seemed pleased with herself, satiated, cat-like, a little arch in her manner. Alex supposed it was because she had got her own way; screwed him in her rival's bed. Not that anyone was really anyone's rival, as far as he was concerned. After all, he never made any promises, nor did he expect any. Elaine was a good lay and a good laugh, most of the time, but if she was going to try to complicate things … He reached over and slapped her rump, not hard.

"*Who* couldn't wait, though?" he enquired. Elaine wriggled against him, still smirking slightly.

"Wouldn't it have been fun if she'd walked in, you know, *during* …" she giggled.

As this was close to his own earlier thought, this brightened Alex's mood, and the flicker of uneasiness disappeared. He kissed Elaine once more, and started to pick up his clothes. Elaine, with a little shrug of reluctance, did the same, rubbing her arm over her forehead, combing her sweat-dampened hair with her fingers.

"I suppose it wouldn't be so much fun if she caught us now," she murmured. "Or do you want to wait a bit longer and see if she comes back?"

Alex shook his head. "Probably better leave it at that. Anyway, I'm getting hungry. You fancy something to eat?" She declined, so he offered to drive her home. As they left, he dithered between replacing the key where he'd found it, pocketing the thing, or leaving it on the kitchen table with a note suggesting that a burglar might do something more than make use of the bed if access was made this easy. Both the latter options, however, necessitated telling Stephanie that he'd been in her flat, and what he'd done while he was there, and there was a part of him that felt that discretion was probably the better part of valour in this case - at least until he had the opportunity of seeing Steph and telling her about it face-to-face. She'd almost certainly see the funny side, but there was no point in precipitating things at this stage. Locking the door, he put the key back on top of the frame and followed Elaine down the stairs and out into the warm summer evening.

FOUR: Who's That Girl?

Stephanie was walking rather aimlessly in the woods, enjoying the summer air, the tickle of the long grass against her legs, the comfortable August heat. The whole encampment of the Tanners gang seemed like some back-to-nature rebel fantasy land, she thought - a fantasy rather than a real primitive village in that no one was going to suffer for lack of modern amenities. Though there was a rather cultivated primitive feel to the place, it was perfectly civilised and comfortable enough, once you got used to it. It covered a piece of land roughly a mile by a mile and a half, enclosed by the fences she'd seen the day she arrived, as well as by the shallow slope which curved round the main site on three sides. The two biggest buildings, generally referred to as bunkhouses, were where most people slept, in a series of partitioned cubicles, and the smaller ones were reserved for the favoured few. Behind these was a block of showers, three in all, and on one side was an immobilised American trailer which contained stores of all kinds and an adequate kitchen; fully electric and as well appointed as it needed to be.

The courtyard area where the bikes were parked usually contained a litter of spare parts, as somebody was always rebuilding or customising something, but behind the bunkhouses was another cleared area, about forty square feet, with a circular fire site ringed in bricks. Every evening the fire would be lit and the entire gang would gather round it, though they seemed to spend the days doing pretty much what they liked. It was rare for everyone to assemble in one place in the day time, though they had made an exception the day Stephanie arrived. She thought back to that bemusing morning, and a little frisson of remembered pleasure and shock went down her back.

Budgie could have warned her what was in store, but maybe it was supposed to come as a surprise; maybe it had been some kind of final test. A few people had come out to see just who was gunning an engine so early in the morning, and when they realised there was a newcomer in their midst, word had gone round in a matter of minutes. Steph had felt unusually self-conscious, been aware that she was blushing, but had decided the only thing to do was ride it out and stay calm. "Let's have a proper look at her, then," she remembered Rocky, the gang leader, saying, and before she had time to protest or even ready herself, Budgie had pulled her dress over her head and let her stand there stark naked before the whole crowd of them. She'd felt an instinctive urge to cover herself, to drape an arm across her breasts, hide her still-damp pussy with her hand, but had forced herself not to move. They wanted to look? Let them look. She had nothing to be ashamed of.

Rocky had told her to turn round, slowly, and he had run a hand down her back and over her bum almost impersonally, as if she were a horse. "See you've warmed her up nicely. Given her a warm welcome," he remarked to Budgie, who laughed and agreed that he'd done precisely that. He'd told her later that sometimes new girls were bent over the nearest knee and given a spank or three by every male member of the gang, and she was glad she'd been spared that. Initially, he had introduced her to everyone as his 'little runaway', and she'd been accepted without question, several of the girls lending her various items of clothing when it was found out that she had nothing more than what she stood up in.

Today, for instance, she was wearing a pair of dark brown, shiny Lycra shorts, with a tight, cropped white t-shirt, her red boots and necklace the only vestiges of her former life. It seemed to her as though the world had contracted entirely, that there was nothing and no one left but Tanners. And it could have been a hell of a lot worse than it was. If the world were to end and maroon her somewhere, she would be less than thrilled with a colony of celibates, or a gang of violent maniacs who delighted in abuse for its own sake as distinct from the subtle blending of pleasure and pain that the Tanners offered her. So far, there had been more pleasure than pain in her dealings with the bikers, as most if not all had healthy sexual appetites, yet never used force, merely asked if she fancied a stroll in the woods, or a "quick slow one". She had never yet felt inclined to refuse, especially as the sex had been straightforward, with little or no spanking or restraint involved. Now and then, sure, someone would take her from behind and spice the final moments up with a flurry of light slaps, but curiously enough, the threat of an increased intensity of stimulation, an escalation of pain, made the pleasure all the sweeter.

She leaned back against a tree trunk, and shaded her eyes with her hand as she glanced up at the horizon - nothing but heat and grass as far as she could see. Her fair skin was beginning to freckle, but she thought the effect quite attractive. She had never been outdoors so much in her life.

Slowly she became aware that there were certain sounds nearby, sounds other than very distant traffic and grasshoppers. Somewhere, not too far away, someone was panting in sexual abandon. Stephanie froze for a second or two, just listening, trying to judge the direction of the sounds. Her breasts were beginning to tingle and so was her sex - always easily aroused, she seemed to begin heating up at the tiniest thing these days. She ran a hand over her breasts, feeling her nipples contract, and slowly licked her lips. Whoever was enjoying themselves - and she could distinguish at least two voices now - was somewhere behind her and slightly to the left. Turning slowly and quietly, she tiptoed through the trees towards the soft moans and sighs, both male and female, that were steadily stimulating all her senses. She remembered reading somewhere, back in what seemed like an incredibly distant former life that, as orgasm draws near, a gun could be fired near the pre-orgasmic participants without them taking the slightest bit of notice. However, she thought, there was no harm in approaching with caution.

A few steps further on, and past a clump of copper beeches, she found the source of the sounds. The two people involved were Patch, a slim, fair haired and rather quiet member of the gang, and his girlfriend, Jade. Jade, with her jet black ponytail, dark brown eyes and large, heavy breasts, a little incongruous on her otherwise thin figure, had made the relationship between Patch and herself very clear on Stephanie's first day, which Steph had found both amusing and slightly annoying, and Patch remained one of the few that she herself had so far had no sexual contact with. Though several of the bikers and girls seemed to be in nominal couples, the majority, as she had swiftly found out, took a rather relaxed view of who could have fun with whom, and there was something about Patch which had drawn Stephanie's attention early on, though she couldn't put her finger on what, exactly. Nor did it seem that she would be putting her fingers on him for the foreseeable future, though he, right now, had his hands well and truly full. Fun was definitely being had, and, as with the rest of the relationship between these two, it seemed to be the sort of thing that was restricted to members only.

Jade, quite naked, was half-sitting, half-lying on a leather jacket spread out on the soft earthy ground. She was playing with her breasts, pulling hard on her nipples and stroking the soft flesh of the breasts themselves. Her eyes were tightly shut and her narrow-lipped mouth open, panting rhythmically and letting out little low moans. Patch was lying between her spread legs, his face pushed up against her pussy, licking her and sucking her, thrusting his tongue into her as his hands moved on her inner thighs. Something about the posture Patch had adopted, the way he was devoting himself entirely to making his girlfriend come, struck a chord with Stephanie, reminding her of scenes from her other life.

Concentrating on the sight before her, she remembered certain glances in her direction from the softly spoken biker, the fact that he seemed to be drawn to her as she was drawn to him - now she understood the implications. Patch, for all he was a member of this rough touch biker crew, had a marked and definite submissive streak which recognised the dominant streak in Stephanie. Jade, silly bitch, clearly didn't know or care about this, one way or the other. Sure, she lay back and enjoyed herself, but neither scratched his back nor pulled his hair. She let out a low howl now, lifting her thighs, tossing her head from side to side, and Stephanie realised the dark-haired girl was coming, and coming quite intensely. As Jade's cries subsided and her limbs relaxed, Patch kissed his way up her body until their faces were level, rolling close to Jade and holding her as she groped for his stiff, straining cock and began to toss him off. Steph, from her vantage point in the bushes, thought it might take more than a quick wank to give Patch what he needed most, but wasn't sure her offer to supply it would be all that welcome. As for the needs building in her own body, the best thing she could do for them now would be to return to the bunkhouse and find someone willing to oblige her with a good hard bone-shaking fuck. It wasn't as if stiff pricks were in short supply.

Having showered, Stephanie was wandering along the track that led to the lower courtyard, wet hair piled up on top of her head. Though it was still warm, the coldness of the shower had made her nipples very prominent, and she knew that anyone she passed would be likely to comment on the fact. The sky was just beginning to redden as a few clouds moved in from the south, and she supposed the fire would be lit soon. It had occurred to her more than once that Tanners would be less of a pleasure zone in bad weather, or in winter; the mainly outdoor life, the lack of central heating and the isolation would lose a lot of their charm if you were soaked and frozen, but for a summer adventure, the basic facilities only added to the sense of enchantment.

"Hey, redhead!" She was on the narrowest part of the path, in the midst of the inner belt of trees, and the voice coming out of the shadows made her jump. She did her best to recover, and swung round sharply.

"What?" she snapped. Jade stepped out between two birches. Wearing Patch's black leather jacket over her own scarlet t-shirt and very tight, faded jeans, she looked tough and almost menacing.

"What do you want?" Stephanie demanded, and Jade put her hands on her hips.

"You leave my man alone, you bitch," she said flatly. "Don't think I haven't seen you looking. You're new here, so you're bottom of the food chain, and you can just leave him alone, all right?"

Steph shrugged her shoulders, doing her best not to

laugh. Of course she wouldn't get involved with Patch if it was going to lead to this sort of aggravation, he simply wasn't worth it, but she didn't feel like giving Jade the satisfaction of telling her so. She simply walked away, continuing in the direction she had been heading, leaving the other to follow her - or not - as she chose. She heard feet running, and noted they were moving away, so she allowed herself a slightly malicious laugh at the other girl's expense. With so many willing and uncomplicated others on offer, she wasn't going to do anything sexual with Patch. At least, she wasn't going to yet.

The fire was blazing brightly when she arrived at the end of the path, and most of the gang were already there. One of the younger girls, Ellen, was putting steaks and sausages on the barbecue, and the savoury smells in the air made Stephanie's mouth water. People were sitting on blankets or the occasional large log, or on battered plastic chairs, drinking beer or wine or cola, eating bread rolls. Steph, looking round for Budgie, wondered what treats this particular evening held for her. Sometimes, the gatherings broke up early, with couples wandering off into the woods or the bunkhouses for a bit of privacy. Sometimes someone would sing, or play the guitar, or a couple would start fucking by firelight in a particularly exhibitionistic fashion, which would usually set off several others and, naturally, if there were any punishments due, they would be meted out in the evening circle. On Stephanie's second night there, two of the girls had quarrelled, which was not in itself a major matter, but they had roused half the gang by screaming insults at each other in the early hours of the morning. They were brought out, stripped, and tied together, face to face, the rope around their hands being looped over a convenient tree branch. They were then soundly thrashed with a leather belt, on their buttocks and shoulders. When both were not only crying but trying to comfort each other, they were untied and generally made much of, kissed, cuddled and fondled by everyone, fully restored to favour.

That had been the most dramatic event so far, though two nights later another girl had been given an old-fashioned over-the-knee spanking. However, that had seemed rather perfunctory as far as Stephanie was concerned. Feeling a slight but definite inclination to see someone suffer, Steph sat down next to Budgie, who was eating a baked potato, and asked if there was anything in particular scheduled for that night.

"Not that I know of," he murmured, splitting the skin of a second potato with one long fingernail. "Mind you, Liza might get herself into some sort of trouble soon. If ever there was a bird completely gagging for it ..." He handed the split potato to Steph, who busied herself with eating the hot, floury flesh, dumping in a slab of butter from the dish proffered by the slim blonde Ellen, circulating now with a winsome smile.

"Does she ever get spanked?" Steph asked, as Ellen moved away.

Budgie shrugged. "Sometimes. You keep on running off at the mouth and you'll be the one getting the spanking."

Having finished his meal, he sucked his fingers clean, reached over and deliberately pulled down Stephanie's t-shirt, tugging it off her shoulders to the extent that her breasts were bared. He began to fondle them absently while she ate, and she felt her nipples crinkle and harden. Glancing briefly upwards as a few sparks flew into the sky from the bonfire, Steph calculated that everyone was assembled. Perhaps, if there wasn't going to be a punishment, there might be some music in a little while, or at any rate, something of interest.

Someone had brought out a cassette player, and now whoever it was changed tapes, and a slow rock ballad filled the night. Jade was prowling round the campfire, still in her borrowed leather jacket and jeans, her black hair loose for once, spilling in a dark cloud over her shoulders. She seemed to be a little unsteady on her feet, and Stephanie half-wondered, half-hoped she would fall over and spill someone's drink or otherwise disgrace herself to the point of needing a damn good spanking.

Some thirty or forty feet from where Stephanie and Budgie were, sat Rocky, the leader of the gang, and Steph was intrigued, if a little wary, when she saw Jade draw near to him and whisper in his ear. If the other girl was sneaking about her, what might happen? Would she find herself singled out for punishment? But then again, she hadn't really done anything, and maybe Jade would be the one who ended up in trouble. Steph had a feeling the rules were at least that arbitrary, but supposed it helped to make life interesting for all concerned.

The lower courtyard was near the slope that enclosed most of the site, and at the southernmost side of the fire the slope jutted out sharply into a natural platform that had been roughly strengthened at some point, shored up with a few wooden crates and planks and fashioned into something that passed for a crude stage. Jade, having finished her conversation, was making for this area, and within seconds she had clambered up onto the platform. Standing there, snapping her fingers to the music that was still blaring from the tape recorder, she gradually attracted everyone's awareness, especially when the leisurely, languid, forlorn song which had been playing was succeeded by the punchy, determined, demanding guitar riff of the old standard, *All Right Now*. People were getting to their feet, moving around to make sure they could see what was going on, and Jade began to beckon and clap her hands above her head, busily calling all attention to herself.

As the music continued, she shrugged off the leather

jacket, caught it as it fell from her shoulders, waved it once above her head and flung it into the crowd. Tilting her hips forward, she drew the belt out of the loops of her jeans, kicking off her sandals and sliding the jeans down her legs. Steph couldn't help admiring the grace with which she freed herself from the tight denim - most people would have struggled or fallen over themselves, but Jade divested herself of her jeans in one movement, neatly kicking them behind her. Now wearing only her scoop-necked red t-shirt, which clung tightly to her wiry body, and a barely-there scarlet g-string, she danced, swivelling and swaying, her face quite impassive, body moving in blatant sexual display.

Budgie had let Stephanie pull up her own t-shirt before leading her forward, probably in complete ignorance of the tension between her and Jade. Now he was holding her in front of him, very close to the makeshift stage, so close that, as Jade thrust her pelvis forward again, Steph could see the faint gleam of sex juice on her thighs, a slight darkening of the crotch of the red panties, and she realised that the dark-haired girl was exciting herself as much as she was exciting her audience. People were whistling and clapping, pressing closer and closer to the edge of the platform.

Jade had closed her eyes for a moment - now she opened them wide and, for the first time, she smiled. She hooked both hands into the neckline of her t-shirt and tore it down the middle, exposing her breasts, the nipples jutting forward eagerly in the evening air. With the t-shirt hanging in rags from her shoulders, she slid her hands, palm-down, into the sides of her little panties and jerked them sharply outwards so the fragile side-straps broke, and the torn scrap of material fell between her legs, a little patch of red on the dusty grass. She shimmied, spreading out her arms and twisting her body and the t-shirt, too, fell away, leaving her utterly naked. The music stopped, and this time did not start up again, the machine's owner probably too absorbed in what was happening to pay attention to his or her dj-ing duties.

Jade pointed into the crowd, glad triumph on her normally sulky face. "You," she said. "You, and you, and you." The four she had indicated scrambled up to join her, ringing her like a wolf-pack, each of them grinning, each of them manipulating their groins through their clothing, strengthening and improving their erections. Circling her slowly, they came to a halt at carefully spaced intervals around her nude, tempting body. Behind her stood Rocky, who might well have been elected leader by virtue of sheer physical size. Standing six and a half feet tall, he was an awe-inspiring figure, hugely muscled, with a bushy, curly brown beard and a head that was completely bald, hands like shovels and crooked white teeth. He unfastened his flies and got out his member, which was as substantial as the rest of him. Jade, with her back to him, bent forward a little and he slapped her bottom once, lightly. She took a cautious step backwards, glancing over her shoulder to place herself properly, and he gripped her hips, easing her onto his erection, sliding smoothly into what must be a well-lubricated pussy. Once she was fully impled, Rocky changed the position of his hands slightly and picked her up, holding her so her feet were dangling and her whole body balanced on his prick. She trembled a little, gasping loud enough for the crowd to hear her clearly as she shuddered in place, held there, contentedly speared.

The two bikers on either side of her - Steve and Duke, Steph thought - moved in close so each was taking some of her weight, groping her tits and pulling on her nipples. Her hands moved aimlessly in the air for a minute, before homing in on each swollen crotch, lowering zippers and grasping the straining cocks behind them. This left only

Patch, who had been standing in front of her, and who now unzipped himself and eased his own prick free of his jeans. He stroked himself with evident enjoyment as he advanced on Jade, who was licking her lips, almost drooling with excitement as she was fucked and groped by the other three men. She tilted herself forward, carefully, supported by their hands, craning her neck and opening her mouth, moaning greedily at the sight of her lover's cock, and Patch gave her what she evidently wanted, sliding into her willing mouth, holding her shoulders so she could wank off the other two men, one of whom was fondling her clit as Rocky pumped her steadily, able to move more freely now she was properly balanced and her weight was distributed between all four of them.

The audience had fallen silent altogether, and all that could be heard were little wet squelching noises, hard breathing and Jade's muffled, gobbling moans. The five of them were moving in unison now, jerking and pistoning, like some multi-legged beast, some creature that smelled sharply sour and sweet, that radiated sex, that reeked of it, that hummed and heaved with it. A tremor went through this composite creature, a deep convulsion at the wriggling pale heart of it, and temporarily it froze to the sound of Jade's smothered cries - "Mmm! Ummm! *Ummm!*" She had come.

Rocky was the first to move independently, pulling out of her and lowering her feet to the ground. Patch then took a step away, his still stiff cock leaving her mouth with an audible plop. Duke and Steve pulled her gently down onto her back and knelt beside her. Her eyes were closed, her mouth open, and sweat gleamed all over her body as they all closed in again. Steve and Duke's cocks were again enfolded in her hands, but this time it was Patch who manoeuvred his way in between her thighs and began to fuck her, with no preliminaries, just short, sharp strokes, balancing on his elbows and thrusting decisively with his pelvis. Rocky, meanwhile, knelt at her head, rubbing his slimy, juice-covered prick all over her face, wanking himself as he teased her with it, brushing the hot, glistening bulb of the glans against her mouth, letting her lick him as he pumped and pulled himself towards his final resolution.

The two on either side of Jade reached their climax within seconds of each other; there were two hoarse cries, their heads went back, and their shoulders slumped. A moment later both moved away, leaving Jade sandwiched between Rocky and Patch, pearls of semen splattering her belly and breasts. Patch, still labouring between her spread thighs, began to thrust even harder as her legs came up and locked around his back. He collapsed forward onto her, gasping for breath, his fair hair matted with sweat. Raising himself, seconds later, he pulled back and then bent over to kiss her navel, and she reached down to stroke his hair as she brought her other hand up to caress Rocky's balls. The gang leader made no sound apart from his ragged breathing, but Jade seemed to sense how close he was. She put out her tongue and darted it across the opening in his glans, a gesture which finally triggered him into shooting thick, sticky jets of semen into her mouth.

Having watched the whole performance in a state of slowly building arousal, Steph had barely realised that Budgie's hand was busy in her panties, until a sharp pinch of her clit recalled her to herself. She jumped and would have moved away, but he had a firm grip of her, and wouldn't let go. She slumped back against him, straddling her legs to make his access easier, aware of her wetness and the demanding throb of her aroused body.

"Come, then," he said almost with an air of boredom, thick fingers moving insistently. "Just come, and then I'll fuck you." She spasmed, jerking against his hand, her knees giving way, and the only thought in her head was a pounding, ceaseless, affirmative - "*Yes!!*"

FIVE: The Game Begins

Just as Poppy had managed to strap the black PVC bustier as tight as she wanted it, the lace snapped on the left side and the garment slipped down, letting her left breast spill out of its straining cup. She swore to herself and tore the thing right off. She supposed it was silly, really, to put on something like that when all she had planned for the afternoon was a simple trip into town, but she had found it and instantly wanted to wear it. Stephanie had so many wonderful, bitch-queen type clothes, so much stunningly slutty stuff to play with. Leather trousers, rubber jackets with hundreds of zips, PVC jeans that laced right up the legs, a tight black rubber dress that moulded to the body, with an oily shine and a penetrating aroma that whispered insistently of sex ...

Poppy was beginning to wonder just how far she could take her little double bluff. Maybe if she teamed the dress with one of the glittery eye masks, she could even per-suade people that she was Stephanie Ames - but could she bring herself to act the dominant? Maybe she could convince them Stephanie had turned submissive - but maybe that was just complicating things too far. Still, she was beginning to want to complicate things, a little bit, nothing too worrying, nothing that would really cause anyone any trouble ... but she was definitely getting a little bored.

She pouted at her reflection in the mirror, topless in a short, tight black skirt and a pair of high-heeled black sandals. She had bought herself three pairs of shoes within days of arriving at Stephanie's funny little flat, but she still resented the fact that none of Stephanie's gorgeous footwear was any good to her. Shiny stiletto-heeled boots in black patent leather, cruel scarlet or purple court shoes, glossy nut-brown boots that laced up to the thighs, a white pair with red flames on the side and laces that would take about half an hour to fasten: all were too big, making her clump around like a little girl playing dress-up in an older sister's things. It was maddening. The fact that a lot of the things she had found were too warm for the extended heatwave was only a minor consolation.

Rummaging in the drawers again she found a pale grey halter necked t-shirt, with the word 'bitch' embroidered in tiny letters on the right breast. She put it on, adjusting the ties of the halter to fit, and admired herself again. Most of Stephanie's wardrobe was scattered around the room, though some of it had been thrown in the direction of the laundry basket, and Poppy was beginning to wonder about buying herself a few new clothes. She was not, after all, short of money, having drawn out a substantial sum from a cashpoint within minutes of leaving her home - no trail of cashed cheques or credit card transactions for Max to follow - but she thought it might prove her independence even further were she to return with a few choice treats for herself, as opposed to nothing at all to show for her little adventure. It really was an adventure, even if she had done very little with her time since she got to this place. Being on her own, making her own choices so entirely, was considerably different to spending her little holiday with Budgie and his crew, where things would not be that dissimilar to life at home. She stalked round the bedroom, trying not to think too much about that - about spanking, punishment, about being roughly taken from behind. She was away from all that for the moment, and anything she got up to now was going to be on her terms.

She crossed the bedroom and peered out of the window. She wasn't really convinced that Max or anyone he might have employed could actually have traced her to the flat, but she did have an odd, gnawing suspicion that someone had been in here recently.

Poppy had always been unable to resist the lure of the sunshine on a Sunday, and so she spent the afternoon in a nearby park with the Sunday papers - partly in the hope or fear of seeing her own name mentioned. She had, after all, been gone from home for a whole week.

When she returned to the flat that evening, it didn't really seemed any more untidy than when she'd left it; nothing had been moved, and if the bed was thoroughly rumpled, well, she never actually got around to making it, or indeed paying it any attention once she had risen from it. What had alerted her was a faint but lingering smell of maleness - of male pheromones. To be blunt, the bedroom gave the impression that a man had been in it, been sexually excited in it, very recently. At first, this had aroused her to the point of masturbation, falling down on the messy bed and frigging herself greedily with her index and middle fingers.

Two orgasms later, though, she had been sufficiently sated to wonder if the scent was real, or just a product of her own randy imagination. If it was real, just who had been in the flat, and why? There were no signs of a break-in, no damage to window or door frames, and Stephanie would surely have mentioned it, if anyone else had a key and was likely to come barrelling in at any point. Finally, she had been able to tell herself firmly that she was simply imagining the whole thing, and had done her best to forget all about it.

Now, back in front of the mirror for a final check, she twirled slowly, admiring herself, the long curvy legs, the pert bottom barely concealed by the short skirt, her red hair in a high swinging ponytail that showed off her elegant neck. She heard the telephone ringing in the living room, stopped pirouetting and stood still, listening, wondering. On those occasions when she had actually heard the phone, and eavesdropped on the callers' comments to the answering machine, she had been relatively reassured to hear that the majority of the calls came from men identifying themselves as either Alex or Paul, the two Stephanie had asked Poppy to reassure as to her whereabouts. It pricked Poppy's conscience, now and again, that she had not taken any steps to do so, but she was reluctant to start anything that might give her whereabouts away to anyone - at least, anyone she didn't know anything about. After all, who was to say that one of these two might not be consumed with righteous indignation at Poppy and Stephanie's joint audacity, and determined to blow their cover for the sake of it?

The voice addressing the answerphone now was male, sexy and softly-spoken, sounding vaguely concerned, and though he hadn't stated his name, Poppy thought she recognised this one as Paul. He didn't sound too pleased with Stephanie's lack of response, either, but Poppy hardened her heart and busied herself with applying a soft fudge-brown lipstick to her full, sultry mouth.

Poppy had spotted the Technocafe on one of her first exploratory forays around Stephanie's neighbourhood, and taken careful note of its location, having thought that its facilities might come in useful. She had not had this particular plan in mind from the beginning, but had considered more than once ways of letting her husband know that she was, at least, not dead in a ditch. Now the first week of her escape had passed, it was time to get in touch with Max, and stir him up a little - after all, she couldn't let him forget all about her. She knew that one of the most infuriating ways she could do this, as well as one of the most untraceable, was via the Information Super-highway, a hobby of Max's that he had never been inclined to share with her. She didn't mind this, as computers held small attraction for her, but knew that he regarded it as very much a male domain, and therefore any fiddling with such things on her part would be regarded as serious provocation, meriting serious punish-ment. Poppy hugged herself briefly, then began to giggle as she left the flat, and headed for the street.

With a large glass of iced mocha topped with whipped cream by her right elbow, and a wedge of sticky, choco-latey sachertorte just behind it, but still within reach, Poppy painstakingly composed her message. The Techno-cafe was all but deserted, with only two male students in football shirts busily downloading pictures of shaven-pussied girls at the terminals furthest away from her. The owner of the cafe had been entirely unsurprised at Poppy's request to send an anonymous e-mail, and had set up the relevant form for her through a secure mailer - he ex-plained all this, though it went pretty much over her head. All she understood or needed to understand was that she should write her message, type in the e-mail address (Poppy had heard Max give it to people often enough) and instruct the machine to send.

The actual wording of the message was proving more troublesome than Poppy had anticipated, though. Her first attempt had been short, consisting of four syllables - 'Hello. Ha! Ha!' - but she had rejected this as silly and, possibly worse, not unmistakably from her. She had then come up with something that sounded like a thank you letter for an unwanted present - 'I'm fine, hope you are too ...' She doubted he was fine, doubted it a lot. She imagined him pacing the Punishment Room, paler and thinner than the last time she had seen him, angrily lashing the empty air with a whip or cane, deprived of her luscious bottom, deprived of her juicy quim, deprived of everything he cared for the most. Poor Max!

She grinned, almost involuntarily, and licked her lips. Now she had it. 'Dear Max,' she typed. 'I told you I would run away, and now I have. I am liberating myself and every one of my orifices. The boys all love me, but not as much as you, so I might even come home. One day. Yours stickily, Poppy.' She gave the command to send the message and sat watching the spinning graphic that indicated her words were being transmitted to Ryanson@Rtower/comm/uk while she polished off the coffee and cake.

She was pleased with the message, but aware that it was not entirely truthful. She had not, in fact, been having sex with hordes of men, having been too wary so far even to engage anyone in lengthy conversation. Well, she'd had some fun with both Budgie and Stephanie, but that had all been a good week ago, and there had been nothing at all since. She told herself she had been slacking, and something she really did have to do before she could go home was to seduce a few more people. She looked thoughtfully at the Technocafe's proprietor, who was leaning on the counter by the till, leafing through a magazine. He appeared to be in his early thirties, olive-skinned with slicked-back, receding dark hair and a shadow of stubble around his jawline; a well-built, solid sort of man, with an air of minor but tangible menace.

He glanced up as the two lads, their lust for sexy pictures presumably satisfied for the present, left the cafe, and his eyes rested briefly on Poppy, taking in the generous cleavage accentuated by the tight top, the bright hair and the pale shoulders. He smiled briefly, then returned his attention to his magazine. A flare of temper blazed up inside Poppy, who was not used to coming second in anyone's scale of priorities. She drank the last of the iced coffee, eyeing the man over the rim of the glass. Then she got up and sashayed over to the counter, carrying plate, glass and little saucer negligently in one hand.

"You finished on the PC, love?" the proprietor asked. "Another coffee?"

Poppy nodded a yes to both, watching him carefully. Something Max had taught her during their time together was that most people had a potential for understanding and enjoying the potent mixture of pleasure, punishment and pain. A few had no appreciation of this complex blend at all, and others were reluctant to try anything new for a variety of reasons. However, those who had a real taste for it often gave their preferences away by means of certain subtle indications. Often these would be spoken, but there were other ways to spot such a person, and an experienced fellow discipline-lover could usually recognise what they were dealing with. For Max, managing such an encounter with a new acquaintance was an elaborate verbal dance, involving the careful dropping of names or key words into conversation, as well as monitoring primitive, minuscule non-verbal signals as they were received. Poppy was too impatient for such a graceful negotiation, but her instincts were telling her the signals were there, discreet but very readable, so she went ahead and dropped glass, plate, saucer and spoon on the floor with a splintering crash.

The proprietor, who had just finished pouring another glass of iced coffee, looked distinctly put out.

"Steady on, love," he said, crossly. "Crocks don't grow on trees."

Poppy hung her head, styling herself into the picture of synthetic contrition.

"Oo, silly me," she whispered. "Sooooorry …"

He looked at her sharply. "I should ..." He stopped, looked again and licked his lips. "Are you always this clumsy?"

Poppy didn't answer, but risked raising her eyes a little to study his general demeanour. It seemed to be dawning on him that something more than a simple accident was taking place, and so far he seemed to accept the way this seduction was being played.

"Sometimes ..." she said. She picked up the fresh glass from the counter and took a long, slow, sensual sip.

"Well, would you mind picking that lot up?" the proprietor said, folding his arms. Instead of obeying, Poppy drank all the second coffee, then calmly let the glass slip from her fingers to shatter on top of the rest of the broken crockery. The man's mouth fell open, but he collected himself sharply.

"You little slag, you did that on purpose!"

She tucked her lower lip between her teeth and gazed at him dumbly, little crackles of arousal running up and down her spine. Her nipples were thrusting hard against her thin top, and she was sure the dark-haired man facing her would have the beginnings of an erection by now.

He came out from behind the counter, moving slowly but with determination, and Poppy waited.

"Pick this shit up," he said as he drew level with her. This time she did obey, bending down to retrieve the shards of china and glass and putting them on the counter, giving him a generous view of her gorgeous bottom in the tight skirt as she did. He stood watching until she had retrieved all but the last few treacherous slivers, then put a hand on her shoulder.

"All right, leave those." When she looked up at him she realised that he was almost, but not quite, smiling, despite the harsh tone of his voice.

"You always this much trouble?" he asked. A warmth

began to spread from Poppy's vulva to the pit of her stomach at the look in his eyes. She had been absolutely right about this man.

"I'm a very naughty girl," she admitted, straightening up. "I always have been."

He shook his head, smiling openly now. "That I can believe. I bet you take a hell of a lot of keeping in order."

"I do, I really do," Poppy said, putting her elbow on the counter and nudging a small glass ashtray full of business cards so that it, too, hurtled to the floor and broke into several pieces.

"Oh dear, I seem to have done it again."

The proprietor said nothing, but went swiftly to the door of his cafe and changed the Open sign to Closed. Turning back to face her, he rested his hand on the bolt at the top of the door.

"Now look here, love. If I'm mistaken here, then all you have to do is say so, and you can get out and go home. I won't even charge you for the breakage's. But it seems to me you want your arse whacked for smashing all that stuff, and I feel like doing just that."

He paused, watching her, and Poppy took a couple of steps towards him, swinging her hips. "People usually do smack my bottom when I'm being a naughty girl," she said, huskily. "I don't know that it makes me any less naughty."

"Well maybe it makes them feel a bit better," he said. He pushed the bolt up, locking the door, and crossed the cafe floor to take a firm hold of her arm.

"Now you come through here with me, and we'll see what we can do about your butterfingers streak."

'Through here' was a doorway behind the counter, leading to a combination store-room and office. On one side were shelves piled high with CD-Roms, mouse mats and other computer paraphernalia, and there were tins of coffee, packets of sugar, powdered chocolate and various non-perishable foods and drinks shelved on the other side. Along the far wall was a narrow bench with drawers underneath it, a couple of newspapers, a small cashbox, a bunch of keys and a radio along its top, and a plain blue plastic chair in front of it. Poppy expected to be put over this swarthy stranger's knee, and was looking forward to the prospect, but he made her bend over the chair, with its back digging into her stomach as she rested her hands on the seat. He opened one of the drawers and took out a rigid plastic ruler, about fourteen inches long and a nasty shade of yellow. Poppy swallowed, a delicious tremor of fear running through her as he showed it to her.

"This is going to sting a bit," he said. "You deserve it, for what you did, and this is definitely a punishment that I'm going to give you. Do you get me?"

She got the message and said so quietly, her breathing becoming fast and shallow. She shut her eyes, listening to his footsteps as he positioned himself behind her, humming faintly under his breath. He hadn't lifted up her skirt or pulled down the tiny scrap of pale blue lace that served for panties, and she was about to suggest - respectfully of course - that he did so, when the edge of the ruler struck the top of her thighs and she squeaked in dismay. The next stroke was lower, on her plump calves, and stung even more, and she was gasping and chewing her lips within seconds as he wielded the plastic again and again against the backs of her legs, stinging, smarting, again and again. It hurt horribly, and she wondered how it could possibly be so bad. Had she softened up, lost all her willpower in only a week without regular sessions in the Punishment Room? She wasn't sure how much of this she could take; not only was it a type of pain that hardly lent itself at all to the delicious, rising crossover warmth that could normally be generated by beating or spanking her

81

bottom, but there was something shaming in this, something deeply humiliating in being punished like this, so dispassionately, so calmly. Unlike Stephanie, despite Poppy's assumptions, the cafe owner was making no attempt to touch her sexually. He simply beat her legs, beat them steadily, not even breathing fast. As she thought about his detachment, though, a seed of pleasure began to sprout in the very essence of her humiliation. She would revel in it, sink into it. She deserved her beating, and she would subvert her deserts by wallowing in this even more deeply.

He stopped hitting her legs and stepped back, and she sighed with some measure of relief, as it had stung more than she would have believed.

"Get up. Turn round and hold out your left hand," he said.

Trembling, Poppy obeyed.

Whap! The ruler whistled across her palm and she squealed, curling her hand round the awful, stinging pain.

"Other hand," demanded her implacable tormentor, and she did as he said.

The second blow hurt even more than the first one, and Poppy felt a tear trickle down one cheek. She sniffed, and wondered whether she was about to cry in real earnest. She wasn't sure it would move this man from his intended purpose, whatever that purpose might be, so she gulped and sobbed, resisting the urge to cry harder. He was still holding the ruler, tapping it against his own palm, and he no longer seemed quite so threatening.

"I think you've had enough of that," he said and she nodded, sniffing again. He smiled, and she noticed that his teeth were very white.

"That's what you get for being a bad girl, though," he observed. He had his hands on his hips, and she saw that he did have an erection, a definite bulge in the crotch of his dusty black trousers.

"Want to know what good girls get?"

"Yes, please," Poppy said fervently, the soreness in her hands and legs diminishing rapidly to the kind of pleasure-glow she loved. He took her by the hips, picked her up and sat her firmly on the bench, then hitched up her skirt and removed her panties in one brisk movement.

"Pull that skirt right up and spread," he told her, and she did as he ordered, trying not to let her sudden raging arousal show on her face. He ran a hand up her thigh in a leisurely fashion, then curled his fingers into her pussy, spreading her labia and smearing the bubbling juices around the hood of her clitoris.

"Good girl," he remarked. "You'd better be good, too."

He undid his trousers and tugged them down to his knees, revealing that he wore no underwear. His cock was stiff, the glans flushed with colour, veins standing out on the shaft.

"I'm going to stick this in you now, and when I stick it in you, you're going to come all over it. Got that?"

Poppy could barely keep still now, such was her excitement. It wasn't that he was devastatingly attractive to her, she thought: he was too coarse, too different from Max - but his bluntness, his almost contemptuous treatment of her was driving her to greater heights of need with every word he spoke. No one had ever ordered her to come before - Max sometimes ordered her not to, but both of them knew this was another way of justifying further punishments if she did.

The cafe owner took hold of her legs and lifted them, draping them over his shoulders, then parted her labia with his fingers and pushed his way inside her wet, grasping, throbbing vagina. His fingers moved up to twirl round her clitoris as he thrust into her, and obediently, Poppy came, nearly hitting her head on the wall behind her as her whole body spasmed. He grasped her shoulders, steadying her as she gasped for breath, and then he began to move inside her, his thrusts measured, his face impassive. Poppy's belly, vulva and mind were in turmoil, little shivery pulses of pleasure running all through her as his firm rod pistoned steadily in and out of her oozing, swollen pussy. She swayed in his grip, her feet flailing as another orgasm reached its peak, making her grind her teeth and whine.

"Hush," he commanded, and she tried to be silent, put couldn't quite manage it. Her legs slipped down as he pulled her upper body forward, still fucking her, still grinding and humping in unstoppable rhythmic determination, and now he kissed her, gagging her with his tongue, but even then she still made a little mew of excitement as she felt him quicken up, tightening his hands on her, digging in with his fingers. He withdrew his mouth from hers and drove wildly into her, pushing her backwards as the bursting, boiling welling of sperm filled her pussy and made her cry out her pleasure for the third and final time.

In the airy, well-appointed office he maintained at home, Max Ryanson faced the woman from the agency across his black oak-topped desk. Miss Hughes was slim and blonde, with cool blue eyes and a trim figure in a pale blue linen suit with a skirt just short enough to hint at something more than frozen efficiency beneath her businesslike exterior. Despite the heat, her legs gleamed smoothly in pale grey nylon - stockings or tights? Max wondered, and almost raised an eyebrow in amusement at himself - to think such thoughts at such a time.

"The agency explained my requirements, I believe," he said, and the woman extracted a notebook bound in blue leather from her navy leather bag.

"You want me to find your wife, Poppy, who's been missing for over a week. Have you got a photograph of her?"

Wordlessly, he passed across the desk the one he had already selected, tensing himself against the flash of pain it caused him to see the wicked little merry face. He had photographed Poppy himself, six weeks ago, lying on the lawn in her green and white polka-dot bikini about ten minutes before screwing her right there on the grass. She had bitten his shoulder, nearly drawing blood, when she came.

He became aware that Miss Hughes was speaking, and made the effort to pay her proper attention.

"Of course, the next step would be to involve the police," she said, and he sighed.

"That won't be necessary, Miss Hughes. My wife has run away. She hasn't been murdered, or run over, or kidnapped by extra-terrestrials. She has simply decided to play truant from me for a while. She left me a note, you see."

"May I?" Miss Hughes interrupted, and Max took the creased sheet of paper out of his wallet and handed it to her. It contained only eight words, but he had read it repeatedly since the night he came in and found it, weighted to the hall table by the whisky decanter.

'Told you I'd go. I'll be back. Maybe.'

Miss Hughes read the note now, and a fine frown line appeared on her forehead. "Mr Ryanson, I hope you understand that I - and you - can't compel your wife to come home if she doesn't want to. She's an adult, and in her right mind."

"I know," Max said, more impatiently than he meant to. "She'll be home soon anyway, but I have to try to find her. She's expecting me to look for her, it's what she wants. I've given her a week, but it's time she came home, and so

I must start to look for her."

Miss Hughes looked puzzled. She parted her soft pink lips and tapped her tongue lightly against her lower teeth, staring at Max, seeming to search for a way of wording what was going on in her mind.

"Are you sure you are in need of our services?" she finally said, and that part of Max which gloried in such things noted that she had lost a degree of her chilly composure, and relished the fact. Now he knew what to do … explain the situation to her in more detail than she might have expected.

"My wife and I have a marriage which is based on a system of rewards and punishments," he told the polished blonde, noting the way her eyes widened at the latter word. "It is not necessarily the case that punishment is exclusively unpleasant, or that the withholding of physical punishment is in itself a reward. Indeed, physical chastisement is in itself both punishment and reward, and the absence of chastisement - by which I mean blows with the flat of the hand, the cane, the paddle or the tawse - can be more painful than the application of it. Nothing is entirely and always what it seems, Miss Hughes."

The blonde's mouth had fallen open, and now she stammered, "You - you beat your wife?"

"Assuredly. If I neglect her, she becomes not only outrageously troublesome, provoking quarrels and breaking things, but she becomes unhappy as well. I don't brutalise my wife, Miss Hughes, I don't beat her up, and that is not why she has run away. I married a girl who enjoys physical chastisement - who *requires* it - because I am a man who likes to apply it. Poppy has run away to provoke me, and because I refused to believe that she would do so. I made a bet with her, that she wouldn't be able to stay away from me for more than a couple of days without calling me to come and get her from wherever she was. Perhaps I underestimated her, I don't know. She has had her couple of days - I have given her over a week now, and I have received an e-mail from her, quite expertly sent through an anonymous e-mailer, by the way, to say that she is alive and well. This whole business is a matter of pride, Miss Hughes."

Miss Hughes crossed her legs with a faint, silky, rustling noise.

"You mean you lose face if you don't find her," she asked quietly. She seemed to expect the comment to annoy him, but it amused him, and he made sure his rueful amusement showed.

"Poppy's pride is what matters more," he said, as gently as he could. "If I make no effort to find her, she will wonder if I no longer love or want her. The fact that I have not yet found her will be upsetting her, because she believes I will be moving heaven and earth to do so. My wife's feelings must not be hurt, her pride and her self-respect matter to me immensely. I will not risk hurting her. Nor will I risk losing her. Do you understand, Miss Hughes?"

She considered for a moment.

"What if your wife is - is involved in another relationship?" she asked, and Max shook his head.

"My wife has a healthy sexual appetite, which I am fully aware of. Infidelity involves the mind and the spirit, not the body, Miss Hughes. I am quite prepared for her to engage in sexual activity with others. That is not my main concern at present - my concern is finding Poppy, and that is why I am engaging your services, to find her."

Miss Hughes opened her notebook and extracted a pen from the spine of it.

"All right, Mr Ryanson. Now where do you think your wife might have gone?"

Max sat back and steepled his fingers.

87

"She has a few friends of her own age - I'll give you their names and telephone numbers, though I have rung them all myself. There's a character called Budgie Barr, who she is quite close to. He rides a motorbike and belongs to some peculiar club, almost a feudal society, or so she tells me. He is quite likely to know her whereabouts, but unfortunately he is not the easiest of people to track down."

Miss Hughes wrote down the information as he gave it to her, and when she had finished and put the leather-covered notebook back in the blue leather handbag, she met his eyes once more and asked, "What will you do with your wife when you catch up with her, Mr Ryanson?"

Max ran his tongue very slowly over his lips, resting his chin on one hand.

"I shall take her to the Punishment Room and teach her the lesson she wants, Miss Hughes. Would you like to see the Punishment Room before you leave?"

Miss Hughes smoothed her hair and stood up in one fluid, graceful movement.

"That would be interesting," she said, and Max noted the slight thickening of her voice with a blend of amusement and arousal. He led her to the doorway of the room with no further comment, and waited for her reaction as she stepped inside and saw what it contained.

He had designed and made most of the furniture himself; the whipping block, the set of stocks, made of cedarwood and painted a deep red, the holes for wrists and neck lined with padded bands of darker red leather; the upright metal cross with its manacles and ankle cuffs of lightweight aluminium. The assortment of whips, canes, cats, paddles and tawses hanging from a rail on the wall furthest from the door had been built up from various sources over the years, and each one had its place and its particular purpose.

Miss Hughes looked slowly round the room, as though noting exactly where everything was. Might she be wondering how it would feel to be strapped down, restrained and helpless, awaiting the fiery kiss of one implement or another? Could she be imagining the sharp bite of the cane into the flesh of her neat, small buttocks? Max forbore to ask her outright. If she wanted any kind of practical demonstration, she had only to ask him. He strongly suspected that there would come a day, quite soon, when she would ask to know more.

SIX: A Taste for Other Worlds

Whether it was because of Jade's warning or in spite of it, Stephanie found she was spending more than her fair share of time around Patch over the next few days. She supposed there was an element of defiance in her behaviour, partly triggered by Jade's exhibitionist foursome - how the other girl had the nerve to claim Patch as exclusively for her own when she would happily gang-bang half the Tanners at once amused Stephanie, and also made her more inclined to take a risk or two.

Every time she encountered Patch, he would be the first to lower his gaze or step out of the way, but she never got the feeling he was trying to avoid her - quite the alternative. She was more and more convinced that he, like herself, had elements of both the dominant and the submissive in his nature. She was careful not to say anything too unmistakable to him, but she would lift her head, tilt her chin, and put a slight but obvious swagger in her walk whenever he crossed her path.

How long this state of affairs might have continued, Stephanie didn't speculate, and then one morning she was distracted from the whole idea when a ripple of excitement ran through the Tanners HQ as word went round that Rocky had received a call to the effect that another gang were coming to visit that evening.

"They're all weekenders, really, part-timers. Straights - not like us," Budgie told Stephanie. "We always give them a bit of a show when they come by, so tonight looks pretty good ..."

A lot of the gang were dispatched to the nearest town centre, to stock up on supplies of alcohol and other essentials. They set off in a convoy, the battered Transit van driven by Rocky and flanked by four bikes, engines thundering as they sped up the slope that led to the road outside. Steph had thought of asking if she could go with them, thinking, with a little guilty twinge, that perhaps she ought to phone someone - Alex, or Paul, or maybe her agent - to say that she was alive and well. There was no accessible phone in the enclosure, though most if not all of the male Tanners had mobiles of their own and she had considered asking Budgie if she could use his, though so far something had always made her hang back. Out in the wider world, she might be able to sneak off for a few minutes. However, Budgie spotted her heading for the van and stopped her with a hand on her chest.

"Maybe not, eh girl? Not this time. You're supposed to be hiding, remember?"

She could see the logic, in a way, but being denied made her reckless. She decided to go in search of Patch, who had not been among the assembling party.

She found him sitting on the raised platform by the fire pit, idly strumming his guitar, and sat down on one of the plastic chairs to listen. He stopped fiddling around when he saw her, and began to play something that she recognised after a moment or two as *Stairway to Heaven*. She didn't speak or even applaud, so he moved on to another tune, and then another, no longer really acknowledging her presence, but she knew he appreciated her being there as much as she enjoyed listening to him in companionable peace. His playing was not the best she'd ever heard; he stumbled now and again, but the soft music in the open air, the rapt look on his face, the golden slanting sunlight, all contributed to Stephanie's warm glow of pleasure, a

91

dreamy feeling that spread languidly through her body, a tingling in her breasts and a sweet, subtle heat in her groin.

Eventually, over his playing, Steph heard the sound of vehicles, and realised that the others were returning. It broke the spell, but she and Patch walked up together towards the main courtyard, reaching it just as Jade, who had also stayed behind, came rushing out of the building where she presumably slept, heavy-eyed and bad tempered.

"What's going on?" she snapped. "Where have you been?"

Choosing to regard the questions as aimed at Patch, Steph walked a couple of steps away, intending to mingle with the returning group and keep a low profile. Unfortunately, before she had got within twenty feet of them, Jade caught up with her in three fast running steps, swung her roughly round by one arm and slapped her across the face.

"Slag!"

Having been generally shy and submissive for over a week, Stephanie almost collapsed into tears, but her former feisty self took over, and she returned the slap with interest.

"Bitch!" she cried. Jade grabbed a handful of Stephanie's long red hair, as though she meant to pull her to the ground. Steph yelped with the pain, but managed to grab the neck of the other girl's blouse, which was delicate Indian cotton in a pale shade of green. She ripped it open, exposing Jade's breasts, simultaneously aiming a kick at her shins. Jade shrieked this time, more in rage than in pain, and struck out at Stephanie's breasts, slapping them as they jiggled in her loose black t-shirt. Steph grabbed one of the belt-loops on Jade's faded jeans and pulled again, trying to swing her off her feet and throw her. Jade let go of her hair, so Stephanie ducked and went

92

in low, ramming her head between the other's breasts and shoving. Jade screeched, kicking out again, and both girls overbalanced, crashing to the ground in a thrashing, yelling heap.

They rolled over and over, snatching at each other's hair, slapping wildly, throwing random punches. As Steph rolled on top of Jade, trying to subdue her by crushing down with her full weight, she was suddenly conscious of the hardness of Jade's nipples against hers - her own t-shirt having been yanked up almost to her neck. Jade was wriggling, but no longer hitting her quite so hard. She bucked, but Steph pressed down heavily. Jade's pupils were dilated, and an idea was beginning to take shape in Stephanie's mind.

Instead of smacking Jade again, she pinched one of her nipples, tugging on it. Jade's hips swivelled, and Steph slid one of her thighs in between the girl's legs, nudging against her pubic bone. Jade's thighs parted easily, and she raised her left leg to rub against Stephanie's crotch in turn. A silence seemed to descend as Stephanie, suddenly burning with arousal, dipped her head and kissed Jade very hard, forcing her tongue deep into her mouth, letting her teeth scrape Jade's lips. Jade used her own tongue to duel with Steph's as she began to squeeze and massage Steph's heavy, aching breasts. Both of them were rubbing their denim-encased pussies hard against each other's thighs, and Steph felt compelled to reach down and fumble, first with Jade's zip, then with her own. Jade's hands were helping her now, and within seconds both girls were bare from the waist down, both pussies hot and oozing juices, sticky and wet.

They rolled again, and Steph managed to swing herself round so that, as they lay on their sides, her quim was level with Jade's face, and vice versa. She felt Jade's hot breath against the folds of her labia, and then a tentative, questing tongue began to circle her clitoris. Wrapping her arms around Jade's thighs, she started to nose and lick and explore her sex in turn. Jade's labia were plump and generous, the left lightly bigger than the right, and her inner flesh had an intriguing, slightly spicy sourness about it. Steph plunged her tongue deeper into the slick, wet opening, using her mouth to fuck the other girl, thrusting with her tongue while she reached round and tickled Jade's anal opening with the tip of her fingernail. The sex-heat was growing fast in her own pussy as Jade kept licking her, licking and licking, concentrating on her clitoris, swirling her tongue around it endlessly and fast. Steph jerked her head backwards sharply, coming in a sudden white-lightning flash that jolted every vertebrae, digging her nails into Jade's backside, barely able to breath for a moment or two.

As the sharp spasms eased, she pushed her face back between Jade's thighs, trying to mimic the swift, darting tongue-flick over the clitoris that Jade had used so skilfully on her. Very soon she felt the other girl shudder and tense, so she gripped her more tightly and stabbed at the little flesh button as fast as her tongue could go. Jade came noisily, groaning and shouting: "Aah, ahh, ahh yeah! Fuck, yeah!" She froze for a moment, hips straining upwards, then slumped. Stephanie let her go, rolling sideways herself, and they sprawled like two starfish, eyes shut and panting.

A deluge of cold water hit Steph full in the face and she sat upright with a screech of protest. Over the rim of a blue plastic bucket, Budgie was grinning from ear to ear.

"Thought you might want to wash the dust off," he observed, and Steph realised that the entire Tanners gang were standing round the pair of them, and had clearly been standing round long enough to watch and enjoy both the fight and the sucking session. She glanced across at

Jade, who had received her share of the icy water as well, and got a rueful smile that matched her own. A temporary truce, at least, appeared to have been declared.

That night even the fire seemed bigger, roaring and crackling, shooting great tongues of orange and yellow flame into the night. Bottles of wine and cans of beer were constantly passing from hand to hand, and the atmosphere grew Dionysian - unrestrained. Shortly before the arrival of the visitors Rocky, frowning portentously, had warned the girls to behave themselves in front of company, and remember who they belonged to, but hadn't been at all specific in his instructions. They were clearly open to interpretation, Stephanie thought as she watched a curvy blonde, Julia, kneeling between the legs of one of the new arrivals, busily sucking him off. Or maybe that was part of the plan - or maybe Julia knew there would be a reckoning later on and was going out of her way to get it. Whatever - Julia didn't seem bothered at all, and Steph wasn't either. She was just enjoying herself.

Rocky was standing on the platform now, firelight gleaming off his hairless skull. Gradually, the conversation dwindled as everyone waited to hear what he might have to say. Stephanie was sitting on a large, old, weathered log, with Budgie beside her. He passed her a bottle of red wine and she drank from it as Rocky proceeded to announce that it was a good night for a ghost story, and to demand that someone get up and tell one.

Though she had mentioned her line of work to Budgie, mentioned her love of storytelling, he had not seemed particularly interested at the time, so she was quite unprepared for him to leap up as he did, indicating her with a cheerfully flamboyant gesture.

"She's got some good ones!" he yelled, and there was a burst of applause. Steph hurriedly thrust the wine bottle into the hands of the black-haired, scrawny biker on her right and got to her feet as Rocky beckoned her forward.

"*Thanks!*" she hissed to Budgie as she passed, but he merely smirked and swatted her buttocks, just hard enough to speed her progress.

"It's the redhead, the little runaway," someone shouted gaily as she got close up to the edge of the stage. One of Rocky's enormous hands closed around her upper arm and he hauled her bodily up to stand beside him. Stephanie wasn't exactly afraid of him, but at close range his big, ferociously grinning face and massive musculature made her feel strongly disinclined to trifle with him.

"Hear you know how to tell a story, Redhead. Got a good one up your sleeve for us?" he asked her, ruffling her hair in a way that just stopped short of being painful, particularly as her scalp was still tender after Jade's onslaught. Still, something about the gesture, part-patriarchal, part-encouraging, sent a rush of adrenaline through her.

"Not that you got any sleeves, mind," he added and roared with laughter. Steph found herself giggling excitedly along with him as she looked down at herself. As all the girls had made a special effort to dress up, she had put on Poppy's turquoise dress again - freshly washed, it looked brand new, and clung even tighter, flattering her figure even more than before.

Rocky, however, was still delighted with his original joke. "No sleeves at all – have you got any *knickers* on, though?" he demanded and, without waiting for an answer, spun her round, flipped up her skirt and displayed to the watching crowd the fact that her bottom was bare.

I don't think there is such a thing as a spare pair of knickers in the whole damn place, Steph was tempted to say, but swiftly thought better of it. The momentary embarrassment of having her naked arse displayed to a whole crew of strangers seemed to kick-start her internal hardware; her reckless spirit rose up and, if she had previously had a few doubts about what kind of story to tell them, they promptly vanished in the wake of this on top of the day's other events - her fight with Jade, the intensely satisfying climax to the fight, the excitement of this party, the shock of being called into the spotlight and, finally, the process of change and awakening that had been going on inside her since her arrival here. The story arrived almost fully formed in her head, and she smoothed her skirt down and licked her lips. This would give them something to think about.

"Off you go then, Redhead. Make it a good one," Rocky said, with a heavy pinch to her left buttock. "Cos if the boys don't like it, you'll have to entertain the troops some other kind of way." He was still smiling as he said this, but there was a definite sexual menace to his words, which put the final touches to the powerful vortex of energy Stephanie felt inside her. Her cheeks were burning and her nipples prickling, hardening against the fabric of her dress as Rocky retreated, and she stepped right up to the edge of the stage. She pushed her long hair out of her face, drew in a breath, let it out slowly, and began.

"There was a biker, riding on his own through the Irish mountains, on Midsummer night. It was full moon, and the road he chose had a lot of bends, twisting and turning as it gradually took him higher and higher into the mountains. He looked down, once, and saw a lake far below, moonlight glinting off the water, and not another human soul or sign of one for miles. He could hear a bird crying out somewhere, a ghostly, lonely sound. Round the next bend, the road opened out, and he saw the ruins of a castle, standing alone in the middle of a sweeping, grassy slope, with further crags and mountains behind it. There was a rough track leading up to what had once been the door, so he decided he would go up there, take a look, maybe rest for a while, so he slowed the bike, took the turn, and got right up to the ruined front door before stopping. He switched off his engine and got off the bike, thinking he would have a look inside the place first, before deciding whether it was a place he might like to rest for the nigt. Now, this man was a man alone, his girl had left him months ago, and he hadn't had any kind of … female company in a while."

Stephanie paused for a moment, checking to see if they were with her. She had feared they wouldn't listen at all, that asking for a story was only a prelude to making her or any other volunteer the centrepiece of a different type of entertainment, but the audience seemed rapt, listening, intent on her words, and she wondered what sort of ghost stories they were used to. She herself was beginning to fly with it, the way she sometimes did at home when a plot was flowing smoothly and fast, an intense, whole-body buzz, throbbing and sparkling through every cell of her.

"The walls of the castle were high, but the roof was long gone, and if he looked up he could see the moon and the stars," she continued. "He went through a narrow passage and out into what had been a great hall. There was a lot of rubble and great broken stones lying around, and there were pillars, broken off at various heights, that made it slightly difficult to see exactly where all the rocks and rubble were. He had a torch, but he had left it in the saddlebags of the bike, he hadn't thought he'd need it, with the moon being so bright. The thing was, he could see something red, something shiny and red, only he couldn't quite make out what it was. He went forward, fascinated, and then, between two broken pillars, he saw her. A girl, dressed in red, in a red silk dress that fitted where it touched, was there sitting on a stone bench as though she had been waiting for him - waiting for a long time.

"She had long, black, curly hair and a pale white face, lips as red as her dress and big dark eyes. Her red dress was cut low, and she had lovely titties, full and firm and white. Her legs were lovely too; long, and pale, and she wore red satin shoes with high black heels. She was the most beautiful woman he had ever seen, and he was utterly lost for words. His mind had almost frozen up, but his body understood. He was getting hard as he stood there, staring at this beautiful vision, wondering if she was real or if she was a dream. She was the first to move, getting to her feet and smiling, and holding out her hands. He took a step forward, and then another, until he was standing right in front of her, looking into her big dark eyes, feeling the thrill of her, knowing he wanted to have her, wanted it more than anything in the world.

"'Yes,' she said, as though she'd read his mind. 'Yes, you can have me. You can have me any way you desire. And everything you do to me, I will do to you. And everything I do for you, you can do for me.'"

Stephanie paused again, watching the quiet crowd. They were listening, she knew, though several had their heads turned away from her, and legs were intertwining, clothes being unfastened, hands seeking breasts to stroke and fondle, fingers curling round stiffening shafts, moist pussies being bared and caressed as she wove the spell of the story around them.

A hand tapped her foot and someone - she didn't see who - handed her up a can of beer. She sipped, glad of the refreshing coolness, cleared her throat, and launched into the story again.

"The pale woman looked him in the eye and asked if he agreed, if he wanted it, if he wanted her. He nodded his head. 'Say it,' she whispered. 'Tell me that you want me - that you want me more than anything in the world.' He said yes, he did, he wanted her more than anything else in the world, and she put her arms around his neck. She kissed him then, and her mouth was wet and warm as it opened for him. As they kissed, he felt her soft, cool hands roaming over his body, peeling off his clothes, and she stripped him naked, there in the moonlight. She stepped away from him then, smiling a little, and then she turned and ran. She ran round a pillar, round the back of the great stone bench. 'Chase me, catch me!' she called. 'Catch me and you can have me!' He ran, dashing after her, bewildered and angry as she flickered like a flame between the pillars, angry at the delay, but turned-on even more by the anticipation, the anticipation of that body, of the pleasures she promised. She ran and ran, shedding her clothes until she was naked too, but then he caught her, caught her and kissed her again. 'Now,' he said, and she laughed. 'Oh, I've been a bad, bad girl,' she said. 'Do you want to punish me?' She pulled out of his arms and bent over a nearby block of stone. 'Do you want to punish my bad, bad bottom?' He realised that he did want to punish her, and with a deep breath, he began to smack her. He heard her counting aloud each time his hard hand struck her pale white behind, and his cock got even harder, and was aching with desire for her. Finally he stopped smacking her, and she rolled over onto her back, lifting her legs in the air, showing him her wet, open pussy. 'Do it hard,' she said. 'Hurt me if you want to.' He fell on her then, and started to fuck her, as hard as he'd ever fucked a woman in his life. Her legs were wrapped around him, and her skin seemed hot to the touch. She kissed him, and then she bit him gently on the neck. 'Remember what I said to you,' she whispered, and he froze. 'Everything you do to me, I will do to you.' She laughed then, and somehow she wriggled, and somehow she was standing behind him and holding him down. She struck him then, she struck his bottom, and her hand was like fire, yet the pain was good, it felt so good."

Stephanie was dimly aware that this might just be the point at which she lost her audience and possibly her pride, but no-one seemed to object to the turn the story had taken. Those who weren't caressing a partner were beginning to caress themselves. Rocky, who had been sitting on the edge of the stage, was now standing beside it, a girl kneeling in front of him, her glossy dark head between his legs. She paused for one quick swallow of beer and went on.

"When she had beaten him, she turned him onto his back, and sank down onto his cock, which was harder than it had ever been in his life, and she sucked him deep inside herself, and held him there. 'You beat me, and I've beaten you,' she said, rocking backwards and forwards, impaled on his cock. 'You fucked me, and I'm fucking you. And what I do to you, you can do to me.' He was moaning now, thrusting up inside her, close to coming, getting closer by the second, and so was she. They came simultaneously, but as she came, she sank her teeth into his throat and bit and sucked, and the pain made him come and come and come, and then she moved her red mouth away and whispered in his ear ... 'What I do to you, you can do to me.' He was beyond thinking or realising, and when she lifted her head and revealed her white throat he rolled her over and pounced on her, dizzily and crazily, and bit her - he bit her, and the blood on his lips was sweet."

Stephanie took another long drink from the beer can, scenting the unbridled, passionate lust in the air around her. Enough, it was enough.

"The biker never went home again - how could he? She had made him like herself. So if you're ever on a lonely road at night and you meet a beautiful girl ... just make sure you're careful out there."

She took a step backwards, rocking slightly on the heels
of her boots, and spread out her arms, lowering her head
in a moderate bow. There was a spattering of applause and
cheers, and in the midst, several groans that really had to
be those of people reaching orgasm. Rocky, who had
clearly finished with the dark-haired girl, moved to stand
just in front of her, raising his arms.

"Well done, girl!" he roared. "That was a blinder! Come
here." She stepped forward, close enough for him to seize
her by the hips and swing her down to ground level. He
kissed her on the mouth and she relished the slight
abrasion of his beard, and the taste of wine on his lips. He
hugged her hard, crushing her breasts against his big
barrel chest, and gave her a spank on each buttock before
kissing her forehead and telling her to run along before
they all wanted a go.

The fire was dying down now. Stephanie skirted the edges
of the gathering, sipping from another can of beer. Her
pussy was throbbing with lust, and she was beginning to
feel petulant and frustrated. Her story had had the desired
effect - arousing them all to the point where everyone was
engaging in some form of sexual activity, but she couldn't
quite see an opportunity for any gratification of her own at
present. She had spent some time sitting directly beneath
the platform, feeling a little drained, but the energy she
had conjured up needed to reach a proper peak in her, as
well as in everybody else. Walking on now, she considered simply lying down and satisfying herself with her
hands, but it wasn't really what she wanted, it wouldn't
fulfil the pounding need inside her. What she really
wanted, she realised as she reached the edge of the woods,
was to take control again, even if only for a little while.

She felt a presence behind her, was about to spin round

when a hand touched her arm. She stopped, half-turned, and saw Patch, alone, bare-chested and smiling.

"Oh, hi," she said coolly, though her heart had speeded up to a jittery, hammering, racing beat, and her pussy was flooded with insistent, painful desire. She began to walk on and he fell into step beside her.

"I liked your story," he said. "It was fine. Turned me on."

"Did it?" she replied, and he took her hand and pressed it to his groin, letting her feel the warm swelling there. No one was near enough to see what was happening between them, and Stephanie stopped dead, looking him full in the face.

"Which bit of it turned you on the most?" At the top of the approximate circle, they could either continue round or turn away from the others, into the trees. Without waiting for his reply, she took a step in that direction.

"Walk in the woods with me?"

He didn't speak, but when she took his arm he let her lead him away from the crowd, into the woods, well out of sight of anyone and everyone. She stopped in the midst of the trees and let go of him, moving up close, almost touching him but not quite doing so. Her breasts tingled, her quim ached, and her mouth was dry with demanding, crackling need.

"Which part of the story turned you on the most?" she hissed, and when he looked away she fastened her hand around his jaw and lifted his face again.

"Was it the part when they switched? Was it the part when the girl beat the guy?" Silence had fallen heavily, but when Stephanie pressed herself against him she could feel his erection, huge and greedy, stretching his jeans. She ground her pelvis against his and wound strands of his long fair hair around her fingers.

"Have you ever been beaten, Patch?" she asked him. As

well as he could. he shook his head. His eyes were very bright. and he ran his tongue across his lips.

"Shall I spank you, Patch? Shall I show you what it's like? It'll be our little secret ..." she taunted, letting go of his hair and dropping both hands to the waistband of his jeans. Still he said nothing, but his eyes showed his raging desire. She tugged his jeans and pants down to his ankles and spun him roughly, pushing him against a tree trunk.

"Hands round this, and stick your bottom out," she commanded, in the neutral tone she always used to her submissives at this point. As he obeyed her, she clamped her thighs together and clenched her fists and the shudders rippled through her - a small orgasm, a preliminary spasm.

His body was pale in the starlit dark, his bottom narrow and smooth-skinned.

She didn't spank him very hard, preferring to err on the side of caution, but as his flesh reddened he began to groan, his face against the tree bark. One of his hands went down to his cock, which had risen even further during the course of the spanking, mild though it was.

"No!" she said sharply. She raked her nails down his back and he groaned again. She took him by the shoulders and turned him so that the tree was at his back. His eyes were half-closed and his breathing harsh as his hand strayed to his swollen cock again. The tree behind him was a sturdy young oak rather than a wobbly sapling, and Stephanie reckoned that it would do.

She kissed him firmly, nipping at his lower lip and raising her right leg as she moved in really close, tilting her pelvis and guiding him with one hand, slowly but mercilessly taking him all the way inside. When he was held tightly in her pussy's grasp, she bit his ear and whispered: "Now we're going to screw, and we're going to do it till I come. If you come first, you have to lick every last drop out of me."

Patch couldn't speak, but he moaned and kissed her neck as she started to move against him, squeezing and relaxing her inner muscles, jiggling up and down on him so that her clitoris rubbed against the base of his shaft and his soft pubic hair. She was so aroused now, so full of pent-up rut that it took less than a minute to bring her off. She found herself pulling his hair again and biting his shoulders almost viciously with the wild intensity of her climax, but the additional pain seemed to work for him too, as he was jerking violently against her, crying out incoherently with release. As the hot flood of seed hit the neck of her womb, Stephanie realised that she could hear further sounds of orgasm, cries and grunts, and that she recognised the voice. She clung hard to Patch in the final tremors, wondering if he, too, could tell that somewhere very close by, Jade was coming her brains out.

SEVEN: The Nights Draw In

It was three o'clock in the morning, and the bedroom was full of candles, their flames glowing still and steady, despite the fact that the windows were open, as the summer night was almost oppressively still. Poppy had taken the precaution of closing the curtains: though her reckless side was tempted to court attention, particularly masterful male attention, she was not anxious to get herself noticed by anyone unsuitable, anyone who might not understand …

Illuminated by the flames, she contemplated her mirror image, slowly turning to view the back of her legs in the hope of seeing some lingering traces of the beating she had received in the Technocafe. Not a single mark remained, and she sighed. Andrew, the proprietor, had told her she could visit him any time she felt inclined, but she could hardly go charging down there in the middle of the night just because she couldn't sleep. She supposed that if she broke into the place and let herself be found by him first thing in the morning, she would receive another dose of the treatment she had so enjoyed a couple of days ago, but then again, there were risks attached to that course of action - what if it wasn't Andrew who found her? Besides, it wasn't really him she wanted, so she would simply have to make the best of what was available to her here and now.

She had been making free with Stephanie's wardrobe throughout her stay, and saw no reason why she shouldn't enjoy Stephanie's collection of playthings just as much. Having rummaged through the antique wooden chest at the foot of the bed that held a selection of items, she had singled out a few things and lined them up on the wooden coffee table, drawing it close to the mirror so everything she wanted was within reach.

She took a long, slow breath and applied a steel nipple clamp, spring-fastened, the little jaws lined with tiny circles of rubber, to her right breast. Her nipple was hard and taut, her body tense with unsatisfied yearning, and the sharp pain of the clamp made her gasp. Setting her teeth, she took the clamp's twin and fastened it firmly onto her other breast, biting her lip and panting as the fierce hurt settled into a steady, bearable, pleasurable ache. Once she was ready, she picked up a fine brass chain, about eight inches long, with quick-release clips at each end, and attached it between the nipple clamps, tugging on it to test herself, moaning a little at the dark sweetness of the sensation this provoked. She walked up and down in front of the mirror, letting the chain swing against her body, feeling the constant soft pull on her nipples. A fine sheen of sweat was blooming on her forehead and upper lip and her vulva felt heavy, swollen and congested. Turning her back on the mirror she bent over and touched her toes, looking through her legs at her reflection, the pink star of her arsehole and the darker pink wet slash of her quim. Both needed attention, needed stimulation, both felt empty, both ached to be filled.

Stephanie owned a nine-tailed leather whip. Poppy held it in her left hand, swinging it in circles and figures of eight. She swished it round, hitting herself across the bottom and finding the effect unsuccessful, tickling rather than striking surely with the kind of sharp, satisfying impact she yearned for. Irritated, she tossed it across the room and slapped herself with her open hand, which was a little better. She might have more luck with the scarlet leather tawse, she conjectured, so she picked that up and tried it against her bum cheek. It made a more satisfying crack as it landed, and gave quite a sting, so she applied it again, and then again, reddening her bottom appreciably. As the warmth of her flesh grew, she abandoned the tawse and turned her attention to a slender butt-plug of polished black rubber, with a wide base and a built-in vibrator. Gazing intently into her reflection's eyes, she began to lick the synthetic phallus, drooling on it, getting it slippery, soft and wet. She bent over again and slowly, gently, carefully, eased the plug into her bottom, little by little, pushing it up inside herself, breathing evenly as she relaxed her anal muscles and opened herself to the latex invader. Only when it was all the way in, base lodged snugly against her skin, did she switch on the little motor. She let herself wail then, wail aloud as the buzzing, churning, grinding sensations made her guts roll and spasm in an almost frightening wave of pleasure.

Her knees were wobbly, and she thought she might fall, but steadied herself. She switched on a second vibrator, this one realistically shaped, a replica of a large, circumcised penis, the head huge and bulbous. Easing herself down onto the floor, she positioned herself carefully in front of the mirror, splaying her legs so she could see her own open cunt in the glass, dark pinkish red and glossy, sopping with her secretions. She ran the loudly humming vibro over her pubic mound and down the soft flesh of each inner thigh while the rectal plug throbbed and juddered in place, pounding at her belly, creating a massive and wonderful turmoil inside her. She began to work the flesh-pink penis into her open hole, sliding it in and out in as realistic a fashion as she could. Her clitoris burned, her stomach turned over, and her breasts were a solid mass of fiery ecstasy.

As she got closer to coming, she yanked the nipple clamps off with one hard pull on the chain that linked them, and almost shrieked at the explosive flash of feeling as the blood rushed back into the compressed flesh in one stunning burst. Opening her eyes again she gazed at herself, aroused even further by the way her labia were swelling and clinging to the big pink prick-substitute as she worked it in and out, in and out, pinching her nipples and wildly kneading and pummelling her breasts, jiggling backwards and forwards on the buzzing black probe in her arse, tears forming in her eyes and spilling freely down her cheeks in the violent, passionate, breathtaking penultimate moments before her whole body was wracked with one huge kicking, jerking, grunting, sobbing climax, so intense she almost felt the flashes of erotic energy discharging like lightning bolts from every hair on her head. She went limp then, flopping down on her back, hips and legs still moving erratically, chest heaving as she tried to fillher lungs with sufficient oxygen, whispering his name to herself over and over again: "Max, oh Max … *Master*!"

When she woke, at about midday, Poppy was still suffused with the well-being generated by her small-hours solo session, but the good feelings began to wear off when she got out of bed, particularly when she found there was no more milk to put in her coffee. Drinking it black, she prowled the flat, kicking occasionally at items that got in her way. Though she hated to admit it, she was beginning to long for her husband. She would have expected him to find her by now. She had proved her point, after all, and stayed away, surviving quite independently, for over ten days. Why had there been no knock at the door, no long, lean, black limousine idling at a corner when she went outside, door on the latch so the occupant could spring from the car and seize her? She screwed up her face and spat the last mouthful of coffee down the sink. "Master, darling, you're slipping," she murmured, and then sat down rather heavily on the nearest of the hard kitchen chairs as a truly horrible thought popped into her mind.

What if he wasn't slipping? What if he had decided not to bother looking for one troublesome runaway wife when there were plenty of other pretty possibilities out there? What if she gave in, called a taxi to take her home and found the door firmly shut in her face and a new beauty installed in her place? The mere idea chilled her to the bone, and she smashed the pink china coffee mug viciously on the floor to relieve her feelings. It helped, but not enough, so she broke two more mugs and a cherry-blossom patterned plate. That was better, and she smiled defiantly out of the window. She'd been too clever for him, that was all. How could he possibly connect her with Stephanie the Scriptwriter, whom she had never met until her first night of illicit freedom? No wonder there had been no signs of pursuit.

Happy again now, her normal high spirits leaping up to their customary level, she decided to get dressed and go shopping. She had worn practically all of Stephanie's clothes now, at least, everything that either fitted or suited her, so it was definitely time to acquire some more.

Late afternoon was sliding towards evening when Poppy staggered up the stairs, two carrier bags in each hand and a new, cartwheel-brimmed black straw hat perched on her flowing red locks.

When someone behind her called out "Hi sweetie," she nearly dropped her purchases, heart hammering, palms suddenly clammy. Half-turning, not sure whether to scream or fling herself into outstretched arms, she realised instantly that the voice belonged to an entirely unfamiliar man - one taller than her but chubby, with cropped, sandy hair and a small moustache.

"All right, Stephie?" he asked, taking a step towards her. Never had Poppy been so glad of a pair of sunglasses - Stephanie's Ray Bans - as she was then. Between them and the hat, the man was unlikely to realise the truth, so long as she got rid of him quickly. Smiling merrily, she told him she had to go straight out again, and scrabbled her key into the door in clumsy near-panic. Once safely inside the flat, she slid down the door, dropping her purchases and doing her best to stifle her wild giggles. Only that morning she'd been practically in tears at the thought that Max wasn't bothering to look for her, yet at the first hint that someone might have tracked her down, she nearly turned inside out with terror. She got up again, shaking her head at her own absurdity. If nothing else, the little encounter went some way to convincing her that she didn't want to go home just yet, after all.

In fact, there was actually something quite attractive about the mystery man on the stairs - a neighbour, she assumed. She wondered if Steph had ever been tempted to further community relations, so to speak, or whether she had been entirely taken up with Paul and Alex, those fretful, phantom voices on the answering machine. Looking at the machine, she noticed that the message light was blinking rapidly again, in a way that indicated a large number of messages. She supposed she ought to play them back and erase them once again, as it was at least two days since she'd done it. She had ignored the wretched thing entirely for the first few days, but when it began to screech persistently, indicating that the message tape was full, she had crossly played it through, scribbling down as many of the callers' names as she could, though a lot of Stephanie's associates had the annoying habit of announcing themselves only as "It's me". In those cases she had settled for writing 'Man, youngish' or 'Woman, Northern accent' or, in one case when she had barely been able to make out anything coherent, 'Bunch of yelling pissheads'.

Oh well, she thought, retrieving a bottle of still-chilled Chardonnay from one of the bags, she would have a nice cold drink while she did this small duty to her absent hostess. It was still very hot, so she took off everything she'd been wearing – electric blue Lycra cycling shorts, a short-sleeved lilac silk blouse that she'd tied under her breasts, and her black sandals, and tossed them over the back of the sofa before opening the windows, pouring herself a glass of wine and pressing 'Play' on the answerphone.

The first message was a cheerful, brief one from someone called Lizzie, who had just got back from somewhere, and fancied "a night out willy-hunting". There were two hang-ups, and a voice saying they had the wrong number, but the next real message was from Alex, the same Alex who had called four times the last time she had played back Stephanie's messages. Previously he had sounded casual or mildly irritated, now he sounded tense, not happy. "Steph, Alex here, Listen, I really would like to talk to you. Owe you a bit of an apology, but I'll explain when I see you. Just call me soon, OK?" He was followed on the tape by the other one, Paul, and Poppy rolled her eyes and stuck her tongue out at the machine. No good carrying on like this, duckie, she thought. It's nothing to do with me.

He really was winding himself up, though. "Stephanie, it's Paul, again. Why aren't you taking my calls? Why don't you ring back? Are you OK? Have we fallen out, have I pissed you off? Look, just call me, all right. Even if it's only to tell me to sod off forever, just let me know you're not dead!" There was a click, and then he was back again, sounding calmer.

"All right, Steph, sorry, that was a bit of a stupid thing to say. I guess you're working on a new commission, you've got your head down. But next time you take a break, call me."

The tape stopped at that point, and Poppy blew a raspberry in its general direction. She found the pen and paper she had used before and added the new set of messages to the list. That Paul really did sound a bit of a wet, she thought. No wonder Stephanie wanted to get away from him. Just like I fancied getting away from Max for a little while. She sighed, her mood shifting. What sort of messages would Max leave on an answerphone for her, if he had the opportunity?

A tiny breeze came in through the open window, and Poppy passed a hand over her breasts, feeling the nipples pucker slightly. *Max.* What was he doing right now? What had he made of her e-mail? She sipped the wine, then set the glass down beside her chair, leaned back and closed her eyes, envisaging Max at his computer, reading her taunting text over and over again, his eyes darkening, teeth gritting at her blatant defiance. A faint pattern of goosebumps rose on Poppy's pale skin as she contemplated the consequences of her husband's anger when she finally returned home.

The only other time she had absconded, she had planned it poorly, taking hardly any money with her and just hoping to find Budgie in one of the pubs he frequented when he ventured into London. She had been spotted on her way between pubs by a business associate of Max's who knew very little of the Ryansons' actual domestic situation, and she had been obliged to feed him some ridiculous story of having lost her purse on a shopping expedition, but at least the man had driven her home, even if he had looked at her strangely ever afterwards.

Max had been full of urbane charm on the doorstep, but once the front door had closed on the departing executive, he had marched Poppy up the stairs in silence, one hand on the back of her neck to steer her, not speaking until they reached the Punishment Room. In there, he had taken a small clasp knife from his pocket and cut off her clothes – the grey stripy shirt and satin bias-cut skirt, the little pale grey camisole, and her matching lace panties, leaving her only her grey satin suspender belt, black fishnet stockings and black suede court shoes. At that moment she had been closer to being frightened of her husband than at any time during the course of their marriage, but even that fear had provided an extra stimulus that flushed her face and swelled her breasts. What was Max going to do?

She shivered a little as he tied her hands behind her back, then put her in ankle-cuffs and sat her on the plain, hardbacked wooden chair that was usually his seat when she was due a hand-spanking over the knee. He fastened the ankle-restraints to each leg of the chair, forcing her knees apart, then drew a length of rope over and under her breasts, round her shoulders and the back of the chair, effectively immobilising her.

"I take it you're tired of me, little slut," he said when she was fully bound. "If you no longer care for my company, then I shall remove myself from your sight for a while." She almost cried, but when he turned to walk out of the room, she caught the faintest trace of a smile on his proud lips, and relief flooded through her. She would be thoroughly and painfully punished, she knew, but ultimately she would be forgiven - was, in fact, already forgiven, but her husband loved her too much to deprive her of punishment.

These thoughts sustained her for a while, but some time later she began to feel uncomfortable, distinctly, physically uncomfortable. She had drunk three large glasses of wine in the course of her adventure and her bladder was now very full. She controlled her muscles, chewing on her bottom lip, but couldn't help wriggling to the extent that the chair shifted, its legs making a grating noise on the hard, wooden floor of the Punishment Room.

Within seconds of the sound, Max was beside her, carrying a long glass of water.

"You must be thirsty," he observed. "I've been unkind, leaving you here with nothing to drink. Here, have some of this." He held the glass to her lips and she looked up at him, eyes warily widened. He nodded once, and she drank steadily, though her bladder seemed to quake as the cold water slid down her throat. Only when the glass was empty was it taken away and put down on the floor behind her.

"How are you feeling, Poppy?" her husband asked her. "Are you sorry for worrying me?"

"Yes," she croaked then, unable to help herself, "Max - Master. I need to pee."

He folded his arms. "Do you?"

She could feel a tiny trickle escaping from her straining insides. Curiously, or so it seemed, the pressure in her bladder was making her vagina pulse and swell, triggering a surge of excitement in the pit of her stomach. This was a new element to their games, but she understood the implications.

"Proceed, then," Max ordered.

"But I - " She writhed against the ropes and he shook his head, almost imperceptibly.

"If you want to urinate, then urinate. Go ahead. You've proved you have no self-control."

With a little choked whimper Poppy tried again to pull free of her bonds, but knew the struggle was hopeless. Relaxing her muscles, she peed copiously, over the chair

115

and onto the floor between her legs. She hung her head as the last trickles left her body, and then Max was beside her, quickly untying the ropes and freeing her ankles from the chair legs. Setting her on her feet, he rubbed her arms and back briskly, turning her this way and that, making sure she wasn't suffering from cramp. He led her over to the free-standing metal cross and fastened her to it with padded leather restraints in place of the usual handcuffs, before fitting her with a blindfolding eye-mask, also of leather and lined with sheepskin. Her vision blocked, depending entirely on her hearing, she held her breath as she heard him moving about, the occasional squeak or rumble as he shifted one or other item of the room's furniture. Then she felt his presence right up close beside her, and his breath against her cheek.

"Now, I'm going to administer a lesson in love and loyalty, little slut-wife," he whispered. She heard him step back, and the heaviest of the tawses blazed across her bottom, the impact bringing a howl of pain from her lips. As the white hot shock began to dwindle to a bearable level, the tails of a leather cat trailed over her shoulder and down to the base of her spine. Then she heard the crack almost before the tails lashed the side of her left breast, bringing another fiery glow of pain to take her mind off her stunned backside. He whipped her breast again, then moved round her to flick the other one, a mass of repeated burning stings, gradually moving to her back and shoulders.

Just as the whip lashes were beginning to blend in the way that took her into and out of herself, opened the gateways of her mind and moved her sexual receptors a level closer to orgasm, the awful tawse bit savagely into her buttocks again.

"That was the second stroke," said Max's voice in her ear. "There are going to be two more before this particular lesson is over." She sobbed, wanting to rub her rump, but unable to move her hands. She heard an odd, chinking noise and shrieked again as she felt something shockingly cold against her labia, an alien intrusive presence, and realised that he had shoved an ice cube inside her.

"Hold it there," he murmured and the tawse struck again, making her jerk violently forward against the cross. One more after this, she thought, one more and he'll screw me, take me down from here, make me come, take me down, forgive me. She felt as though she were made of fire, cold fire, burning and freezing, the ice in her pussy melting against her molten flesh, her bottom a furnace of pain, sweet pain, her breasts glowing with heat, her mind humming and singing with almost pure sensation. She waited long minutes, but the fourth blow didn't fall, and then she felt her husband pressing against her back, naked now, his arms round her, groping and pinching her breasts, his cock hard against the cleft of her buttocks, hard and warm and determined.

"Do it," she sobbed. "Screw me! Take me now! Take me hard!"

He chuckled, and withdrew from her. She moaned, at first with disappointment and then in renewed pleasure-pain as the soft-tailed cat began to flicker across her shoulders again. Gradually the intensity of these blows increased, but now she was fully open to them, open to the hot soreness, breathing loudly and rapidly, nerve-endings buzzing, sizzling, delicious sensory overload coursing through her. Water dripped between her legs onto the floor, and there were his fingers again, seeking and finding her aching clit, frigging it so hard that she screamed a full-blooded scream, hurling herself back-wards and forwards, orgasming once and then again, a chain reaction of climactic explosions almost pulling her body out of the bindings. At the very peak of her resolution, the moment when all she could see with her blind-folded eyes were brilliant shapeless flashes of colour and she could barely hear her own cries through the pounding of the blood in her ears, the tawse fell one final time across her arse cheeks, and he screamed again and slumped forward, crying bitterly, crying with relief, and release, and contrition.

Max untied her then, removed the blindfold and picked her up in his arms, kissing her wet face as he carried her out of the Punishment Room and up the stairs to the big, luxurious bedroom where he laid her down on the bed and took her slowly, gently and tenderly, in the traditional missionary position they generally only employed once a year.

The shadows were lengthening, and Poppy's eyelashes were wet by the time she'd finished her reverie. She lifted her hand to her mouth and licked it clean of her juices. Funny how easily that memory brought her to a climax - a session like that was not one she'd like to experience every day. She picked up her glass and drained it before padding into the bathroom and switching on the shower, feeling sweaty and sticky, yet still restlessly excited, over-stimulated and not fully relieved. She wanted a cock, she thought, a real cock, a warm flesh and blood one to do what a plastic imitation or indeed her own fingers could not. She still didn't feel quite brave enough to go to a pub or a club on her own, looking for a man, so she would have to make do with substitutes unless some inspiration struck. Perhaps if she phoned for a pizza later, maybe this time they would send an attractive delivery boy.

In the gathering twilight Paul walked along the street to the block of flats where Stephanie lived. His deadline for copy-editing the new training manual was the end of the week, and he was nowhere near on schedule, but today had been a total washout. He'd been unable to work for fretting obsessively over Stephanie - where *was* she? Why the hell hadn't she returned any of his calls?

His section head had sent him home at two o'clock when he invented a migraine as an excuse for slumping at his desk with his head in his hands, but even the generally sympathetic Judith Wallace would hardly believe in a four-day migraine.

Of course, it wasn't the first time he'd let pleasure take precedence over work - the Monday he and Steph had decided to take an extra day to finish off their weekend with some extremely kinky friends had been the time when Stephanie had elaborated an absurd but enjoyable fantasy about Judith Wallace metamorphosing into some archetypal dominatrix and putting him over her desk to give him a good caning for dereliction of duty and the rest. The idea of the polite Ms Wallace, with her hand-woven skirts, ethnic bead jewellery and untidy chestnut perm, striding around her cosily-cluttered office in skin-tight black leather had provoked alternate surges of laughter and lust, but no daydream or conceit like that would comfort him now.

He reached the front door to the block just as that crop-haired squaddie type who lived on the top floor was coming out. Recognising the man, Paul nodded.

"Looking for Stephie?" the neighbour asked blithely while Paul tried and failed to remember his name.

"Yeah," he said, in the end. "D'you know if she's in?"

The neighbour shook his head, shrugging, his smile undiminished, and Paul struggled with an urge to punch him.

"I saw her a couple of hours ago, but she said she was going out. She's been in and out a fair bit this week. Busy lady."

"Mmm, yeah," Paul managed as the man went cheer-fully over to his car and got in, switching on the radio to a loud blare of dance music before roaring away, smoke jetting from his exhaust.

Paul contemplated ringing the bell anyway, but decided against it, not wanting to make any more of a fool of himself than he already had done. It was clear enough now that Stephanie no longer wanted to know him. She wasn't dead, she wasn't mysteriously missing, she just wasn't interested in him any more.

He walked slowly back the way he'd come, smacking one fist into the opposite palm at intervals. One of the things he'd always liked about Steph had been her direct-ness, her honesty. At least, he'd seen her as direct and honest, but if she could ditch him like this, she couldn't have been the girl he'd thought she was. Dropping him without a word, cutting him right out of her life for no apparent reason, was a cowardly thing to do - a cruel thing to do. He suddenly wanted to have her in front of him, but not in her normal, sensually superior mood. He made himself imagine her naked, on her knees, hands roped together, begging for the chance to apologise or make it up to him. His cock burned with frustration, but the vision faded away, and he made his way miserably home, totally uncomforted.

EIGHT: Party Harder

Sitting on the edge of the mattress, with the tattered quilt thrown round her shoulders, Stephanie shivered, feeling chilled, despite the fact that the fine weather still showed no signs of breaking. Her head was whirling with a mixture of conflicting emotions: anger, fear, embarrassment, guilt and what she supposed was a kind of homesickness. This is what it all comes down to, she thought, this is the bottom line, this is for real. What am I going to do?

This thing, this shock, this crisis, had happened about half an hour ago, when she'd been messing around with Ellen and Liza and a couple of the lads from the other gang, who were staying on for a few days. A water fight had been in happy, hysterical progress when Budgie had appeared and told her to come with him immediately. Most of the usual mischief had gone from his face, and she'd felt a sudden sinking in the pit of her stomach. He had said nothing more to her until they reached the smallest of the bunkhouses, where Rocky generally slept. The gang leader had been sitting on the porch steps, arms folded, face impassive, and behind him leaning against the wall, looking nastily pleased with herself, was Jade.

I might have known the little cow wouldn't let it lie, Steph thought crossly. By the sound of it, she was loving every minute when it actually went down, but she doesn't respect any of us in the morning, I guess. Now what? Do we both put our case and the winner gets to spank the loser, or what?

Rocky, however, asked her no questions and didn't give her a chance to say anything at all. He simply told her, quite calmly, that she was getting above herself and needed to learn a lesson about her place in the scheme of things. Therefore when the fire was lit that night, she would be tied up in public, and anyone who felt like it would be entitled to punish her. Subsequently, anyone so inclined could make use of her in any other way they saw fit. That would teach her how things stood around here. Oh, and by the way, he added, looking at her brown Lycra shorts and matching t-shirt, she should wear something pretty. The last was said with enough of a smile for Steph to wonder if the whole thing was a joke, but it clearly wasn't. The interview was terminated, and she was dismissed. Budgie, who was supposed to escort her out of the Presence, looked like he had something else to say to her, but Stephanie couldn't bear to hear anything, and had simply bolted, heading almost blindly for the corner of the far bunkhouse that had pretty much become her space by default, and now sat biting her lips and wringing her hands.

The shivers were subsiding now, and she took a succession of slow, deep, even breaths. Sorry, Poppy, she thought, but this is as far as I go. Game over. She resolutely fought down the tiny little inner voice that kept suggesting that this semi-ritual of pain and penetration had a sleazy attraction all of its own. It had been fine to flirt with the idea of exploring her submissive side - an interesting little experiment that Fate had provided - but this was going much too far. She pushed back her hair and tried to make sensible plans. She had very little money, and no real idea of where she was, so getting home might pose a bit of a problem. She supposed she could simply flag down a passing car once she got to the main road, but there might be awkward questions and, whatever the outcome, she had no wish to cause trouble for the Tanners who, after all, had taken her in and thoroughly entertained her up until now. Probably the smartest thing to do would be to find Budgie and throw herself on his mercy.

Just as she was getting to her feet, however, Budgie himself appeared, still looking relatively serious.

"You all right?" he asked, standing in the archway that divided this cubicle from the next, effectively blocking her exit. She shook her head, aware of a possibility that she might be about to burst into tears. Swallowing hard, she began to outline her options for getting off Tanners property and going home. Budgie heard her out, then flopped down on the mattress, putting his arms behind his head.

"Thought you had more guts than that, girl," he remarked, and Stephanie gaped at him.

"What?"

"You always bottle out when things get a bit tough? You never looked the type."

Limply, too amazed to speak, Stephanie dropped back down beside him, clutching her head.

"I thought you'd help me," she said, finally. Budgie took out a cigarette, but didn't light it.

"I would, if you were in a real mess," he said. "But you ain't. You're just chickening out."

Now she found herself getting angry. "Hang on, I'm not chickening out! You heard what he said - that anyone can beat me and then they can do whatever else with me - they could - they can -"

He laid a finger on her lips.

"I heard him. But what do you think they're gonna do that's so bad? You ain't about to get pistol whipped, or have some nutter break your legs or anything. It's a spanking, girl. OK, it's a big spanking, but you can take a spanking. Then when you've had your spanking, you get laid. You like getting laid, and you've had just about everyone here before. What's the big deal?"

Stephanie could hear that inner voice again, the one that had been whispering lustily about the joys of total submission, tempting her with vivid images of exactly how it would feel. The voice was louder now, a filthy little insinuator that dared her to take it on, to accept the challenge, to do it thoroughly. She felt a tiny leap and flutter between her legs and looked at Budgie again. He had lit his cigarette, and was blowing smoke rings, gazing at her through them, the sparkle of wickedness back in his dark eyes.

"Don't you want to show us what you're made of, *Stephanie*?" he said, and she gulped. He hardly ever used her real name, and somehow this got through to her. Rocky had not ordered something awful beyond imagining, something dreamed up out of a wish to cause cruel and unusual suffering; this was a challenge, a quest, a test, the true heart of her adventures. Before coming to this place, she had never submitted sexually to anyone, had hardly even thought about what it would be like to place herself in that rôle, but now she was facing abject, absolute submission, and how well she performed under the foreordained onslaught would be a matter of pride as well as of possible pleasure.

"What will they do with me, really? I mean, who gets to spank me, and how many of them, and then what?" she murmured, not looking directly at him. "I mean, you must have seen this sort of thing happen a time or two before, and I would like to know what I'm getting."

Budgie exhaled smoke, and Steph glanced round, seeing the slow smile spread over his face.

"Well, let's say I have and I haven't seen it done. Every time's a bit different, if you get my drift," he said. The feeling of warmth and wetness in her sex was growing noticeably now. She drew her legs up onto the mattress and lay down, rolling over to snuggle closer to Budgie, who took another drag on his cigarette.

"Go on, tell me more. I mean, will they hit me with their belts, or with their hands? Will everyone screw me, or just a few of them?" Even saying the words was affecting her, quickening her breathing, stimulating all her senses. Budgie grinned.

"Seeing as you're new, you won't get much more than hand spankings, maybe a paddling or two. Duke might paddle you, he likes that. And a fair few are gonna fuck you, especially in your arsehole. You're getting it for being uppity, see? So they'll do you up the back door, that's the best way."

Steph nibbled her lower lip. Somehow, she had thought this might be on the agenda. For a moment, she shuddered with unease, but then she remembered Poppy's moans of delight and passionate climaxing when Budgie had penetrated her anus during that brief interlude by the tube station. There was obviously something to recommend the practice.

"What's on your mind now?" Budgie asked, suddenly. He leaned over and crushed out the last inch of his cigarette on the bare floorboards. "You got that look about you, like there's still a few more questions. Ask away, girl, only I ain't got all day."

She raised herself on one elbow and glanced down into his cheerful, sinful, twinkling eyes.

"The only thing is, I've never had it that way before," she said. "That's what bothers me - I don't know what to expect."

"Really," he murmured, stroking her back, his hand moving down to her bottom to squeeze the plump curves. "Want a little test drive, do you? I reckon I can handle that."

She touched his cock through his jeans - ordinary denim today, stretching slightly under the pressure of his excited organ - feeling the heat of his skin, hard and aroused. She didn't speak, but began to caress him through the fabric, slowly manipulating the thick, firm flesh as he stroked her bottom, then tugged down her shorts. He started to slide his index finger up and down the cleft in her buttocks, in a motion that was somehow soothing yet very pleasurable. Gradually, he worked his way down until he was just touching the tightly puckered ring of flesh, and she moved her thighs warily, lifting the upper one to allow him better access. He made no attempt to push into her bottom immediately, just rubbed it gently, his finger circling round and round the tight, tender little hole until she relaxed into the caress.

"Lie face down," he whispered and, when she obeyed, pulled the skin-tight shorts right off her. With her face against the pillow, she listened to him unzipping the pockets of his leather jacket and remembered the lubricant he'd made her use on Poppy, to ready her bottom for penetration.

Moments later, she felt soft, wet coolness on her own bottom and through the smooth chill of it a steady, gentle probing.

"Open up," he coaxed. "Come on, open wide, that's it." It was easier than she'd anticipated, but strange all the same. Her pussy and her clitoris felt awakened, needy, yet not unbearably so, not yet, and she raised her rump slightly as he withdrew his fingers from her and shifted position. She felt his cock touch her anus, the pressure, the blind seeking of it, and willed herself to relax as he slowly moved inside her, a little at a time, gentle but unstoppable and, though her stomach was churning, her quim was burning now, burning with lust, and she wondered how soon she would climax. He slipped his hand underneath her, feeling for her clit, moving a little faster in her bumhole now, his own breathing hoarse and uneven. The combination of his fingers and his fat cock was driving her wild, and she moaned loudly, turning her head to one side to let the pleasure out in cries and grunts as she began to climax, aware as never before of the rippling, clenching, quivering tremors in her whole pelvis; vulva, perineum and bottom. Budgie sighed, jerking against her, and she felt the warmth, the wetness, the hot spurts of him coming inside her.

Liza and Julia were the ones who led Stephanie round the perimeter of the fire to the stage area, and she was glad of that, glad Jade hadn't formed part of the escort. These two had come to get her early in the evening, bringing some clothes for her, things she hadn't seen before: a white PVC skirt, very short, fastening with a zipper from waistband to hem at the back, and a very low-cut white lacy vest. She was no longer really sorry to find herself in her present situation; though one part of her mind was still quailing a little, another part of her felt pleasurably tense, sticky-dirty-slutty glad about it all, and underneath was a detached little something reminding her that, all else notwithstanding, there was material here for a screenplay and a half.

Still, the absence of a gloating, triumphant Jade was a definite positive, Stephanie thought as she scrambled up onto the platform she had stood on to address the masses the previous evening. Front centre now stood a whipping block, rather old and battered but sturdy enough; the familiar folding-leg structure, with its pad of cracked, oiled black leather and supple leather cuffs for wrists and ankles oddly reassuring, though the box beside it, containing a jumble of pain-inflicting instruments, was less so.

Rocky was standing to the left of the stage, his face almost a blank canvas which chilled her momentarily. However, when he turned to take her arm, his expression was briefly averted from the quiet, intent audience and, to Stephanie's amazement, he winked at her. That one gesture dealt with the last lingering worry that what was about to happen to her would involve any serious brutality, and she submitted quite calmly to being bent over the block, hands and feet buckled into the cuffs, bottom raised and facing the crowd. Probably winking at them as well, she thought, with a quick flash of irony as her zip was pulled down and the little skirt fell away - Liza had cautioned her against wearing panties and she had not bothered to point out that she had none anyway.

Face down, pulling gently at her bonds out of sheer nervy restlessness, Stephanie listened to her own rapid breathing, as the momentary bravado disappeared, and wondered how long this awful, silent anticipation was going to last. There was no music and not even a murmur of conversation, and her mouth was dry again, her mental barriers beginning to crumble. Why didn't somebody say something? Why didn't they start? Anything at all would be better than this, the flickering shadows of firelight, the odd upside-down view of things she had through her own parted thighs, and this tense, taut, expectant silence.

Just when she thought that she would have to start screaming, simply for the sheer relief of hearing the noise, screaming without a single blow having landed on her bottom, Rocky stepped in front of the stool, his tree-trunk legs blocking her view of them all, and spoke.

"You know what we got here? We got a girl who doesn't know her place. We got a girl who needs a lesson in respect. We don't let girls go around needing lessons and not getting 'em at Tanners, do we?"

The roar of the crowd was unanimously enthusiastic,

but Stephanie barely had time to take it in before Rocky's massive hand made a ringing, walloping connection with her bare left buttock and she yelped, choking off the cry then doubling it as he hit her on the right side, balancing the powerful blaring pain with equal measures. She could almost see the picture in her mind, two glaring scarlet handprints on her soft, pale skin, and drew in a long, hissing breath between her teeth.

There were footsteps on the platform now, and Rocky was telling them to get in line, get in line, wait their turn, stop pissing around. They were lining up just out of her sight, and she wasn't sure if this was good or bad - she had no idea of how many gang members would take up an opportunity as tempting as free use of her bottom, and maybe seeing the actual number would frighten her or, indeed, disappoint her.

A hand touched the base of her spine, a smaller hand than Rocky's, and she peered through the gap that framed her only field of vision, but the plimsolls and jeaned legs she could see were unidentifiable. The hand continued to feel her bottom for a moment or two, then began to pat it lightly all over, as though blotting wet ink. The sensation was distinctly curious on top of the fiery impact of Rocky's two distinct swats, but the pattering got steadily faster and firmer, culminating in four sharp slaps that definitely registered, before the unknown punisher walked away.

The next one, who arrived barely seconds after Mr Pitterpat, had a double handed approach and gave her ten on each cheek, neatly spaced, firm and somehow satisfying. He paused, and Stephanie let out a long, shuddering sigh, wondering what the next in line might do. She could hear the audience now, chattering and whooping in occasional exhilaration, but then the double spanking recommenced and, after a further ten on each side, her bottom was beginning to glow quite thoroughly. Someone else arrived and proceeded to lay a powerful dozen on her right side, and she whimpered, feeling unbalanced suddenly, one buttock sizzling under the impact, the other feeling almost cool. Luckily, whoever followed this participant evened her up with six sharp blows from a distinctly calloused hand on her left bumcheek, and she twitched a little, breathing hard through her nose.

There was a change in the tenor of the watchers' vocal contribution and she tried to work out what they wanted.

"Yeah, right!" she heard Rocky shout. "You got it. Next one up, something from the box!"

What? she thought with a flash of alarm, then understood, and shivered. Her bottom throbbed hotly, yet the pain was not unpleasant, rather the reverse; a fiery tingling ache that was affecting her quim as much as her arse.

Close by, she could hear the rattle of whips and canes being sorted and picked over, and her thigh muscles tensed in anxious anticipation. Heavy, buckled boots stomped into position behind her, and something smooth and hard and quite large was laid against her bottom, then withdrawn. It seemed to have a similar surface area to a shoe, yet felt as if it were made of wood. Steph had seen wooden paddles before, but had glibly dismissed them as too traditional for her own personal tastes. This one descended with a kick like a mule and she shrieked at the huge, explosive pain, shrieked again at another thunderous impact, another and another, and she dug her nails into the wood of the whipping block and roared her distress into the night.

Whap! Whap! Whap! Each blow was a separate, distinct horror, each one contributing to a cumulative riot of feeling, on and on and higher and higher, pushing her further than she had ever imagined possible.

It probably didn't last as long as it seemed to, but when the paddling was over she hung limp and trembling, her bottom one white-hot blaze of shock. She tried to analyse how she felt, but her mind seemed entirely fragmented, the world nothing more than a vortex of fiery pain, a supernova, all the heat of the universe concentrated in her battered buttocks.

There seemed to be a respite of some sorts, a brief interval as she sagged over the block, head spinning, eyes wet, and then into her blurring vision came a hand holding a light, slender wand of wood. The hand looked like Budgie's, and when she turned her head he was crouching beside her, showing her the implement.

"Switch for a switch," he said, very quietly, and grinned at her, raising his eyebrows before getting to his feet and walking round to the designated place. Stephanie tensed herself, wondering how much more this unassuming little item would hurt her already so thoroughly marked and punished flesh, determined nonetheless to stay the course, to ride it out, to shout and scream as much as she had to but never, never to beg for them to stop.

She shut her eyes again, waiting for the first strike, and felt a thin line of stinging fire lash across her upper thighs. The next stroke fell almost on top of it, and those that followed on in a lightning fast succession all the way up and down the plumpest part of her backside set up a stinging, sizzling pain that seemed to flow through her body in waves of warmth, bright and glowing, a hot prickly rush that was different to the unmitigated anguish offered by the wooden paddle. Her nipples began to hurt now, only it wasn't a real hurt, more like a deep itch of frustration and, as she twisted her head helplessly from side to side, she became aware that her quim felt congested, heavy and definitely aroused. The switching continued and, almost involuntarily, she strained to move her thighs wider apart, rocking unsteadily on the leather pad, trying to give her clitoris some extra stimulation. This time, when the blows stopped falling, she actually whimpered in protest, and heard laughter close behind her.

"Think she's ready for Part Two? I do!" someone - she couldn't tell who - shouted joyfully, and Rocky growled an assent.

"Shall we grease her up, then?" he asked the crowd. They loudly agreed that they should, and it became a chant: grease her *up*, grease her *UP*, grease her *UP!!*

Her coppery hair fell damp and sweaty over her face, into her mouth. Her bottom burned and her whole body felt tense, jumpy, nerve-endings sizzling and crackling all the way through her, but when someone slapped a great handful of some sloppy, slippery, chilly stuff across her rump and began to rub it in, she bucked and groaned with desperate lust. Whoever was applying the cream had a merciful streak, and promptly thrust two fingers in between her puffy, pouting labia while strumming her clit with another. Stephanie yelled and came, tossing her head up and down, all her muscles heaving and jumping. Before her convulsions had done more than slightly diminish there was a long, slender cock nosing its way into her well-creamed, oozing, punished backside, and she pushed backward eagerly to meet it, to engulf it. He came quite fast, but when the next took his place, someone else bent down and untied Stephanie's right hand, lifting it and guiding it to her wet, hungry pussy.

"Frig your cunt," a voice instructed and Stephanie, a mass of physical demands, all conscious thought spiralling into nothingness, did exactly that, rubbing and pushing madly, fingers squelching in her dripping maw.

She had no idea how many cocks she took, was barely aware that at least two people were holding the legs of the whipping block and keeping it steady as she masturbated herself, coming and coming, ceaselessly convulsing, multiple orgasms like fireworks across the sky, behind her eyes, hard thrusts deep into her bowels, spunk trickling down her legs, the shouts of exultation and grunts of satisfaction all around, hearing her own cries, long ululating moans, the whole world seeming to tilt on its axis and fall into a million points of light ...

Stephanie felt someone gently easing out of her, an affectionate pat on her still-throbbing bottom, and then a deluge of water, surprisingly warm, mostly over her bottom, oddly soothing, and a little more over her head, bringing her muzzily back to awareness. Then they were untying her legs and her other hand, lifting her to her feet, and wrapping a leather jacket round her shoulders as they held her up and turned her round, Budgie on one side of her, Rocky on the other, holding her tired arms above her head like a prize-winning fighter. Everyone was cheering, bellowing their approval, and she knew she was grinning like an idiot, barely capable of understanding anything said to her.

Rocky kissed her on the mouth, his beard tickling her face, and when he released her she staggered and nearly fell. Budgie scooped her up then, carrying her in his arms like King Kong carried Fay Wray, and she let herself go limp, head against his shoulder as he took her back towards the bunkhouses, back through the crowd of smiling faces.

"I'm so sleepy," she mumbled as the firelight dwindled behind them, and Budgie chuckled.

"I ain't surprised. Well done, girl, you done us all proud. Poppy as well. You're a right little star."

"I am?" Stephanie murmured, closing her eyes. She thought she had probably never felt quite this relaxed, so spent and yet so satisfied. Before they got through the bunkhouse door she was fast asleep in Budgie's arms.

"As far as I could gather, all this took place last night," Miss Hughes was saying. "However, I distinctly heard one of them refer to a person they described as 'Budgie's red-headed bitch', and I assume that means this man Barr whom you mentioned the last time we met. Furthermore, I think it would be logical to assume that the red-headed woman described is your wife, Poppy."

As she finished speaking, Max felt a relief so great it was almost nauseating. Poppy was alive and well, and safe in the hands of Budgie Barr and company, who would not let her come to any harm. He closed his eyes briefly and passed a hand over his face. He had to clear his throat before carrying on the conversation.

"You actually made your way inside the Tanners place then. Do they not post guards, or something of that nature?"

Miss Hughes raised her eyebrows. She did not look as though she had just returned from what Max couldn't help thinking of as an updated outlaw encampment, never having been there himself, but only heard about it from Poppy, for whom the place had seemed to hold an unholy fascination.

Miss Hughes was wearing a grey and white checked suit, the short-sleeved jacket open over a white silk vest, the only incongruous note being her slightly grubby white espadrilles, which were probably her one concession to both the heat and the rural environment she had just visited on his behalf. She appeared to be a little put out by Max's question.

"I saw no guards, Mr Ryanson," she said, coolly. "Mind you, there would be no real reason for them. They own the land they live on, quite legitimately. I believe it was once a holiday development that fell out of favour. I did not explore the place in any detail - having overheard the

134

conversation I have just related to you, I thought it best to make my way back here and report my findings. I also thought it advisable to avoid making them aware of my visit if possible. But I am reasonably convinced, both because the red-haired girl was described as being in the company of Mr Barr and also, given our previous conversation, the nature of the - um - activities they suggested this girl had engaged in ... well, as I say, I am convinced that your wife is with these people."

Max believed her, believed both her honesty and her accuracy, but his relief and joy made him mischievous.

"I'm not altogether clear on the subject of activities, Miss Hughes," he said softly, and the private detective bit her lip.

"Would you care to describe them to me?"

She met his eyes, and Max controlled the urge to smile. If she did as he asked, he would know it was safe to proceed a little further. He held his breath for a short while as Miss Hughes looked at the floor, twisted one ankle round the other and smoothed her skirt before replying.

"Well," she said eventually. "Well, as far as I could gather from the conversation, bearing in mind that I was crouching behind a bush and some twenty or thirty feet from the speakers, it appears that the girl to whom they were referring had been spanked and whipped in public, and moreover, had enjoyed it. She also appears to have ... um ..."

She wasn't looking at him, so Max was able to study her unobserved. Even though she would undoubtedly be wearing a bra underneath that pretty white top, her nipples were twin hard points against the fabric. Still, he wanted to make her continue, so he pressed a little further.

"What else, Miss Hughes?" he asked her softly. Miss Hughes did look at him now, checking his expression.

What she saw appeared to reassure her in some way, and she began to speak again.

"It appears that the girl allowed several of the men present to engage in sexual congress with her, in front of everyone else," she said primly.

Max nodded. "That sounds like my wife. Chastisement arouses her considerably," he observed, before deciding that Miss Hughes was ready for the next step along.

"I believe a great many women find chastisement arousing. In fact, Miss Hughes, I am inclined to believe that discussing the subject arouses you."

She gasped, and hot colour flooded her face. She might get up and run away now, he thought, and if she did, he would let her go, though he was excited himself, firm and rigid and ready.

She didn't get up, just sat still, quite still, looking at him, cheeks pink, lips moist. Finally she said: "I've never tried anything like that. I don't know if I'd like it or not."

She looked doubtful, almost embarrassed, and he wished she were close enough for him to pat her hand in the time-honoured reassuring manner. He did it verbally instead, keeping his tones warm and moderate.

"We could, of course, engage in a small experiment, if you wish," he suggested.

Deeper colour washed over her face, and she nodded, just once. She made a move to get up, and he pushed his chair back from the desk, allowing himself room to manoeuvre.

"If you would like to come round here, my dear …"

She obeyed, dumbly, hanging her head, so charmingly unsure of herself.

"Now, over my knee, that's it …"

She was smaller and lighter than Poppy, though not by much, and he took a moment to delight in the feel of trembling, compliant female over his lap as he gently and

136

carefully raised her expensive skirt, revealing white, filmy but generously cut panties. He stroked her bottom through the soft fabric and murmured, as much to himself as to her: "An even dozen to begin with, I think."

He didn't lay them on very hard, but she was gasping by the fourth, sobbing at the seventh and squirming blissfully as the last two landed. He dared a finger inside the silky white panties and found her decidedly moist.

"Does it arouse you, Miss Hughes?" he enquired and she answered in the affirmative, and loudly.

"You can get up," he told her, and when she did, he rested his hand lightly on his visibly erect penis. She nodded her head again and slowly pulled her panties down.

Minutes later, with the elegant detective rising and falling astride him, sunk exquisitely deep in her velvety honeyed warmth, Max wondered if he should refer to the fact that not all detectives were as punctilious about taking down their particulars. His balls contracted, ready to shoot out his seed, and he decided that this was no good time to be frivolous.

NINE: Missing You

The Rod and Lantern was a rougher pub than those Paul usually frequented, and he couldn't help wondering what Stephanie had made of it on those occasions she'd been there. If she'd been there at all, of course; it was perfectly possible that she had lied to him about that, along with everything else. Still, he had exhausted all the other possibilities, and he could only hope that this, the final option, would somehow bear some fruit.

Even at one o'clock on a sunny Saturday afternoon, the single bar was dark and gloomy, with three heavily tattooed men playing darts at one end, and a group of belligerent-looking pensioners discussing the racing round a table by the door. As his eyes adjusted to the gloomy light, Paul spotted Alex sitting on his own at the bar, filling in something that was probably a pools coupon. Nothing ventured, nothing gained, he thought coldly, and made his way over.

"Alex. How's it going, mate?"

Alex looked up quickly, heavy-lidded eyes widening as he realised who was addressing him.

"Not seen you in here before," he commented, and turned back to his coupon.

"I'm looking for Steph," Paul said, loudly enough to earn a frown from one of the darts players. Alex put down his pen and paper and made a moderate show of looking all round the room, even underneath his own barstool.

"Can't see her, pal. She's not here. Hasn't been for a

while, in fact."

For a moment, Paul was horribly tempted to punch the other man in the mouth, and it took a considerable effort to squash the impulse down. Glancing at Alex, he noticed something which made the urge for violence die away - for all the sneering bravado, Alex looked strained, short on sleep, and none too happy. He was clearly suffering as well.

"She's dumped you, too, hasn't she?" Paul said, and sat down, heavily, on the nearest stool. "Have you any idea what we did to piss her off?"

Actually hearing it put into words gave Alex a curious sick feeling in the pit of his stomach. He had phoned Stephanie several times, not too worried at first when she failed to return his calls, but after the Sunday he had taken Elaine to the flat, it had begun to bother him rather more. He had mostly succeeded in burying his rising hurt and unease, partly because his conscience bothered him, and it was not that difficult to assume that Stephanie had some-how found out what he'd done, and was sufficiently unimpressed to … well, to not take his calls for a while. However, though he could just about believe that Steph would disappear from his life after nearly eight months of good friendship and great sex, he had always assumed that she had something approaching a 'proper' relation-ship with Paul. If she was treating her short-arsed blond to the same silent vanishing act, then maybe there was another explanation, a reason other than a callous or outraged cutting of ties.

He picked his drink up and downed the remainder of it in one gulp.

"Whatever's going on, I'm sick of it. Come on, let's go and sort it out, once and for all."

Paul followed him out of the pub obediently enough, but

paused on the pavement to ask where they were going.

"Steph's flat," Alex replied. "We'll just go straight in and ask her what she's playing at."

"She won't let us in -" Paul began, and Alex rolled his eyes.

"So we'll let ourselves in. Now get in the bloody car."

It took Paul most of the drive across town to work out a tactful way of demanding to know how come Alex had a key to Stephanie's flat when he himself did not, and he was still not sure of how to phrase it as they stormed up the stairs to the cream front door. When Alex reached up and deftly flicked a key off the top of the doorframe, he was glad he'd kept his mouth shut.

He half expected Steph to come yelling out of the bedroom, cursing the pair of them roundly for barging in on her and turfing them out with orders never to return, but within seconds of crossing the threshold and arriving into the messy living room, he could tell there was no one there. He leaned back against the door, despair nearly robbing him of the power to speak, though, curiously, there was a sharp, sudden pain in his loins that he normally associated with passionate arousal.

Alex had gone to check the other rooms, running from one to the other in a frantic but rather hopeless fashion and when he returned, Paul forced himself to stand up straight, assuming that they would simply leave. Alex, however, was shaking his head in bewilderment.

"You ought to see this," he said, spreading his hands. "You really ought to - I mean, I don't know what the hell is going on here …"

"What *now*?" Paul snapped.

"The mess!" Alex continued. "Look, she was always messy, but nothing like this. The bedroom looks like the fucking Oasis tour bus - well, if they were a bunch of transvestites maybe. Just look at it, look for yourself."

Without any real interest, sick at heart, Paul followed him back into the bedroom and realised that he did have a point. Stephanie had always been inclined to toss her clothes on the floor, especially if she was removing them prior to some spectacular or even some fairly ordinary sexual frolicking, but she usually straightened the place up every two or three days. Now, though, clothes littered every available surface, were crumpled on the floor, slung over the back of a chair or half-off their hangers, swinging from the open wardrobe door. Shoes, too, were scattered around, and Alex picked one up; a high-heeled scarlet slingback, with a pattern of raised silver studs across the toe.

"Take a look at this," he said. "Seen it before?"

"I don't think so," Paul acknowledged. "No, probably not."

Alex snatched up another shoe, and threw it across the room at Paul, who caught it, aware that this was one he did recognise. It was a purple patent leather court shoe, high and angular, and Paul held it lovingly, remembering the times she'd made him kiss it. The leather was shiny and cool, and he stroked it, sliding his hand up and down the heel, aware of the faintest traces of her scent clinging to the lining, imagining her foot neatly encased in it, tapping across the room or resting on his balls. He realised Alex was speaking to him, and looked up, embarrassed.

"What?"

"I said, what size is that shoe?" Alex repeated, grimly.

Still stroking the smooth, beautiful patent, Paul was bemused by the question, but answered it anyway.

"Seven."

Alex weighed the red shoe in his hand, looking at it with dislike.

"This is a five."

"So?"

"So this isn't Stephanie's shoe. It wouldn't fit her."

"Oh, come on," Paul said, still puzzled. "Maybe she bought the wrong size, or maybe she bought those red things for someone else."

Alex threw the scarlet shoe down, and wiped his hand down the side of his black jeans.

"Like fuck. You telling me she doesn't know her own shoe size? And that's not all. There's a half-empty bottle of Chardonnay in the kitchen."

"Chardonnay? She doesn't drink white wine," Paul acknowledged, and Alex half smiled.

"Specially not Chardonnay, she said once it tastes like rat piss, and she'd rather drink rat piss, at that."

"So what are you saying?"

"I don't know yet. But I know there's someone else been here - and someone else is living here."

"Someone who's got small feet and drinks Chardonnay," Paul reiterated softly. He looked again at the purple shoe in his hand and suddenly hurled it at the wall, shaking with rage.

"So she's gone dyke, and that's why she's dumped us!" he snarled. "That's it, isn't it?! She's moved this Chardonnay-drinking bitch in here and dropped everyone else, just like that, just like we were nothing to her!" He could hardly get the words out, and thought he might even be about to cry. Either that, or smash the flat, smash everything in sight. Alex was looking troubled, shocked, and Paul contemplated smashing him in the mouth, too, just for good measure.

Alex wasn't sure quite what he felt, but he thought Paul's conclusion ridiculous. There was definitely something strange going on, but the flat didn't have the feel of a newly-feathered love nest, and he doubted that the explanation they sought was anything like that simple. Plots of films involving changelings, murders and even alien abductions flickered through his mind, but he did his best to dismiss them. He began to prowl the room, looking for clues, but watching Paul out of the corner of his eye. He had a feeling the other was about to snap and do something really stupid, but could think of nothing to say that might calm the situation down. Paul was still standing there, breathing hard, and suddenly he did erupt, whirling round and slamming his fist into the wall, marking the paintwork and probably hurting his knuckles.

"Bitch!" he yelled, and Alex crossed the room in two strides and grabbed his shoulder.

"Pack it in, all right? What good's that do?"

"Sorry," Paul mumbled, looking embarrassed. "What are we going to do, though. What the fuck are we going to do?"

Alex rubbed his eyes, wishing his head would clear.

"Well, for a start, we're not leaving. We'll wait until someone comes back. Someone's got to show up sooner or later. At least if we wait we'll get some sort of an answer."

He thought back again to being here with Elaine, the previous Sunday. Had there been anything different about the flat then, any sense of strangeness? Should he have waited a bit longer, or even left a note? He didn't know, he could not honestly recall anything that had really struck him as unusual, but then he had been very keen to get on with satisfying Elaine - and himself. He thought it was probably not a good time to mention the incident to Paul, who had now sat down on the edge of the bed, head in hands. Though he looked abjectly miserable, he had lost that air of potential violence, for which Alex was grateful.

"Come on, Paul, mate," he said. "We might as well

have a coffee while we're waiting. Go and stick the kettle on."

They were sitting in the kitchen, which was at least reasonably tidy, sipping cooling coffee, when they heard a key turn in the lock, the door open, and someone come inside. Alex glanced at Paul, nodded once, and they both rose from their seats, stepped smoothly through the doorway into the living room, and stared in amazement at the pretty little redhead who was staring back at them.

Poppy, having been to the corner shop to indulge a craving for strawberry ice cream, and then been unable to decide between strawberry-vanilla, fraises-des-bois or frozen strawberry yoghurt, had been singularly cheerful all day, but her good mood splintered the second she saw that there were two men in the flat. The bag containing the tub of ice cream fell from her limp fingers and she froze, back to the door, too stunned to turn and run away. They seemed equally stunned by the sight of her, and she rapidly discarded any idea of their being Max's emissaries. That left only one other option, and with the realisation, her fear fled and her normal impish confidence returned. With a little sniff of petulance, she straightened up, flicked back her hair and put her hands on her hips, thrusting her breasts forwards.

"OK, which one's Alex and which one's Paul?" she asked.

"How the -"

"Never mind." The blond one looked ready to pick a fight, but the other one cut him off sharply and took another step forward. "I'm Alex McCoy. Who the fuck are you?" he said.

Poppy assessed him, rather liking what she saw - rather liking the look of the fair one as well, come to that. Stephanie had taste, evidently. One dark and sort of sinister in a very sexy way, the other blond, clean-cut and very attractive as well - lovely! But they didn't seem to be in the mood for any kind of naughty fun with her - not right now, anyway. Perhaps she'd better try to be obliging.

"My name's Poppy," she said, then added, for good measure. "I'm a friend of Stephanie's."

"Fine," Paul said, also moving towards her. "Then perhaps you'd like to tell us where the hell she is, and where she's been for the past couple of weeks." He was certainly direct, but Poppy was feeling full of mischief. They needn't look so stuffy or try to scare her, she would tell them in her own sweet time if she told them anything at all.

"Actually, I wouldn't like," she returned. She bent down and picked up her ice cream.

"What I'd like to do right now is eat ice cream. Would you like some?" They stared at her in open-mouthed silence, but neither made any move to impede her progress into the kitchen, where she took a bowl and a spoon from the dish-drainer, served herself a nice big helping of ice cream, and sat down on one of the chairs, crossing her legs at the ankles and letting one sandal slip half-way off her foot. They were still gaping at her when she dug the spoon into the moist pink mound and began to eat, and she felt mildly irritated by this. All right, so they'd been roundly outwitted by a couple of girls, or at least kept guessing for a fortnight, but there was no need to get all upset over it, was there?

Ice cream alone was not the most seductive of foods, not as suggestive or as easy to eat in a meaningful manner as, say, a banana, or a spear of asparagus dribbling hollandaise sauce or melted butter, but she did her best with each spoonful, slowly closing her lips over the smooth pink scoops, sucking the delicious cool cream lasciviously into her mouth and licking the spoon clean each time with little cat-like dabs of her tongue.

"Sure you wouldn't like some?" she asked them after the final spoonful, as neither one had moved a muscle. The blond one, who appeared to be the more volatile, actually clenched his fists for a moment as he demanded, through clenched teeth: "*What have you done with Stephanie?!*"

The pretty redhead put the dish down then, and smiled at them with creamy lips.

"I haven't buried her in the back garden, you know. She's perfectly all right. She's just doing me a favour."

Though she was a teasing, wicked little witch, there was a calm conviction in her words, and Paul felt some of the tension leave him. He still didn't understand what was going on, but at least he was reassured that Stephanie was alive and well - and whatever this maddening, pixie-like creature might have done, she did not look remotely capable of inflicting serious harm on a feisty girl like Steph.

What Alex was thinking, Paul didn't know, as he turned towards Paul and gave him a swift wink. He couldn't tell if it was reassurance or conspiracy until the other stepped into the kitchen and leaned against the sink, just close enough to Poppy to impress upon her how much taller than her he actually was.

"You've done something, though, haven't you?" Alex said, with vaguely threatening sweetness. "You're the reason for whatever's going down - for why no one's seen Steph for about a fortnight, and she isn't answering any calls - it's all down to you, isn't it?"

The girl gazed up at him through half-closed eyes, slowly licking the last traces of pink ice-cream from her full, sultry mouth.

"Maybe," she said, then grinned. "She's all right, you

know. Oh *do* stop being so scary about it."

Paul felt a flicker of annoyance at her silliness, but at the same time, something about the brattish act coupled with the beautiful breasts, that lush hair so much like Stephanie's, and that adorable, mischievous mouth, was beginning to turn him on. Alex, however, still seemed cucumber-cool in every respect.

"You think we're scary?" he asked. "We haven't even started on scary yet."

She tilted the chair onto its back legs, balancing on her pointed toes, and widened her big brown eyes.

"You wouldn't do anything awful to me," she breathed, and then shook her head and wrinkled her nose, kittenishly. "No, of course you wouldn't. Boring!" She let the chair fall forward into place and crossed her shapely legs again, rotating one foot in the backless silver sandal.

Such dainty little feet, Paul thought, with a sudden mental image of those small feet kicking and flexing in delight as they crossed around a man's heaving back. He blinked and shook his head as the girl tugged up the sliding straps of her pale grey, floaty little slip dress, printed with lilac flowers, and alternated her bewitching smile between the pair of them. Alex was still watching her steadily, and suddenly he reached out and caught hold of her shoulder, not hurting her, but gripping her firmly.

"Come on, out with it," he said. "Where's Steph? Where is she?"

Some girls, Poppy reflected, might have been alarmed by the turn events were taking, but she was entirely delighted. Partly, she was fully aware that these two men, however much they might want to know about Stephanie, were not going to torture her for the information. Well, they were going to persuade her to talk, but only in a manner that would make it fun for all three of them.

Mainly, however, she had a phrase in her mind, a phrase that seemed to be strobing there, outlined in neon; a phrase that filled her with a sense of ecstatic well-being. The phrase, which encapsulated the solution to everything, was Honourable Surrender. It implied a settling of the game, an acceptable draw, a way of returning to normal with no feeling of loss, or of giving in. But to be truly honourable, she thought, with a little prickle of excitement running the length of her spine, it would have to be hard won. Her skin tingled lightly, all over, and she sensed a definite charge to the atmosphere, a building tension, a feeling of readiness, a quickening in her sex and in her mind, and decided to turn the power levels up a little further.

Alex's fingers were digging into her flesh, but his hands were warm and strong, and felt good to her. She set her feet on the floor and pushed herself upwards until she was standing, tilting her head up with her naughtiest expression.

"What will you do if I don't tell you?" she asked, pertly. Alex appeared to consider the situation, and actually looked taken aback, less able to cope with her than he had originally indicated.

"Smack your bottom?" he eventually said, with a slight but discernible hesitation.

Poppy stuck the aforesaid portion outwards and wiggled it. "Oh, really?"

"No." Paul hadn't meant to interrupt, but the last thing he wanted was for Trouble-in-a-minidress to regain the ascendant. He crossed the kitchen and put his hand under her chin, turning her face so she was looking at him. He was no longer really anxious, nor particularly angry, and his own wicked streak had resurfaced as a favourite theory of Stephanie's suddenly reoccurred to him.

"No," he repeated. "That won't work. She wants her

arse walloped. She likes it. If we give her a good hiding she'll just get all damp-knickered, and enjoy herself, and she won't tell us a thing."

Though he doubted Alex was a mind-reader, as he looked at a loss at first, the dark-haired man was clearly willing to play along.

"I take it you've got a better idea, then. Need any help?"

"Sure, bring her into the bedroom." Paul said, heading in that direction. "Carry her if she won't co-operate."

Alex grinned wickedly, scooping the girl up and throwing her over his shoulder. Though she wriggled and kicked, he carried her into the bedroom and tossed her on the bed, with its rumpled satin sheets.

Paul was already pulling silk scarves out of a drawer and rolling them expertly into soft, fat ropes. The head-board of Stephanie's bed had two smooth, rounded wooden posts on either side that were ideal for this purpose - and frequently used for it, he thought as he fashioned two reasonable nooses and lashed the squirm-ing, struggling girl to the bed-head by her wrists.

"Feet as well?" Alex suggested, dodging a kick, and Paul nodded, tossing him a couple of longer scarves.

"Bed legs," he said tersely.

Alex looked mildly affronted. "I *know*!" Paul grinned and Alex returned the grin as he tied each of Poppy's ankles to the legs of the bed, which had no suitable baseboard. She lay there, spread-eagled, rolling her head from side to side and wriggling her hips. She was still fully clothed although her dress, riding up, revealed that fully-clothed was really a matter of wearing a dress, and nothing else - she wore no panties.

"What shall we do with her, then?" Alex wanted to know, and Paul sat down on the edge of the bed, smiling slightly.

"There's one thing I've heard about girls like this," he

said, very softly. "They can take any amount of spanking, but they also tend to be very, very ticklish."

Poppy's mouth fell open, and she looked ready to scream, so Alex thoughtfully closed the window and drew the curtain across it while Paul lightly skated his fingers up her calf and tickled behind her knee. His hand moved up her left inner thigh a little way, then over to the right thigh, working back down to the sensitive skin behind the kneecap. Meanwhile Alex, going with the flow, had sat down on her right, and lifted her dress right up to her neck, laying bare her smooth, creamy-skinned body. He began to tickle her ribcage and belly, using both hands yet hardly touching her at all, just skimming her with the very tips of his fingers and stirring her senses almost beyond bearing.

At first she shied violently away from the tormenting hands, but they followed her every movement, mercilessly, relentlessly, and she began to giggle and then to shriek, thrashing madly, almost lifting free of the bed, choking and spluttering, little squeals and sighs escaping her as the two men tickled and tickled, butterfly light yet impossible to ignore, impossible to endure in stoic silence, impossible to keep still for. She had no breath to speak, no will-power to form coherent words, yet in the depths of her wailing, stammering near-hysteria, she could feel herself warming, opening, moistening, as the insane stimulation continued.

When she was scarlet-faced and whooping for breath, Alex and Paul stopped what they were doing and looked at each other, sharing a smile of slightly cruel satisfaction. Poppy, between them, continued to gasp and struggle, and they waited until her breathing had become a little more even.

"Are you going to tell us, then?" Alex asked as she finally let out a long, shuddering sigh and quietened. She opened her eyes, which were wet with involuntary tears, then squeezed her mouth tightly shut and shook her head.

"Maybe we'll have to beat her," Alex said, mock-sorrowfully, and Paul bent over the bed, put a hand lightly on Poppy's neck, and held her still.

"Oh, I don't think so. Like I said, that's what she wants. I think there's other ways of getting what *we* want."

"Well, that one didn't work," Alex grumbled, but winked at Paul again, and Paul realised that he was trying to confuse the bound girl, almost playing good-cop-bad-cop with her, and smirked.

"What's plan B then?" Alex was asking him. Paul laid his hand over Poppy's eyes, so she couldn't see, and slowly mouthed his idea in as few words as possible. Alex watched, reading his lips, then let out a short laugh.

"Good idea, mate," he said, and nodded once for emphasis. "Shall I start, or will you?"

Paul just grinned, taking his hand away from Poppy's eyes. She looked up at him, warily, but not apparently inclined to fight or object. She was enjoying herself so far, which was fine. He and Alex were, to an extent, enjoying this means to an end as well.

Using just his index finger, Paul traced a line down her throat and then around her breast, circling it once, then circling it again, a little higher up. Alex, on her other side, began to draw a similar series of concentric circles around her right breast, until both their fingers were moving slowly round and round her dark brown areolae. She gasped, jumped once, then lay still, muscles tensing slightly. Her nipples had hardened, crinkling up tightly, forming into little protruding peaks. Each of the men then held their fingers to her mouth, pushing gently until her lips opened, then slipping their fingers just inside, wetting them with her saliva, then returning to the slow, subtle tracery of her breasts. They circled the nipples themselves now, occasionally flicking each hard little bud, and Poppy began to whimper softly, her thighs moving ceaselessly, restlessly, driven by the evident, mounting need in her sex.

Sharing another conspiratorial grin, they changed positions slightly. Paul lay down beside her, kissing each aroused nipple in turn, sucking on them quite firmly, noting the rosy blush darkening her skin, while Alex began to caress her inner thighs, stroking softly rather than tickling this time. She moaned, and he moved his hand to her vulva, which was moist and swollen now, the flesh darkening with her steadily increasing excitement. He stroked her labia, very gently, very carefully, feeling her wetness, turned-on by it almost in spite of himself, caressing her expertly, stroking and stimulating, steadily working her up, but neither penetrating the hot, pulsing slit nor touching her hard, protruding clitoris, even though she was mewling and thrusting her hips upwards, curling her toes and clenching her fists. Paul was still noisily attending to her breasts, slurping and kissing and smacking his lips against the soft skin.

Alex slid his fingers slowly down the sides of her vagina again, this time tickling the sensitive spot between her quim and her anus, and her thighs tensed and quivered.

"Oooooh, God!" she moaned. "I'm going to come, don't stop, I'm going to come."

Instantly, as though they'd been doused with cold water or zapped with a cattle prod, both Paul and Alex pulled sharply away from her, sitting upright and folding their arms. Poppy squealed with outrage, and jerked her body from side to side, pulling on the scarves that held her as they sat impassively on either side of her.

"What are you doing?" she wailed. "You can have me, you can do anything - please!"

"I don't think so, darling, " Paul said placidly, as Alex

brushed his palm over her taut nipples once again.

"I don't think you really want us to play with you any more."

"I do! I really do!" Poppy gasped, writhing desperately. Her body was quivering, every nerve-ending and synapse frantic for the rushing, explosive convulsion of orgasm that hovered just out of her reach. She hung on the brink; unable to go on, to break through, to explode.

"Please, please, make me come, please do it, please touch me," she begged, almost incoherent with frustration. She had momentarily lost track of the game, of the stakes, utterly at the mercy of her burning body, her gushing, demanding, aching sex.

The two men were both smiling, practically laughing at her, stroking her breasts again, keeping her at fever pitch, yet neither of them would give her that tiny extra touch, that little push she needed so badly. She wailed, tossing her head on the pillow as the cruel-but-kind touching went on; hands kneading her breasts, and two warm, wet mouths licking and sucking her shoulders and the hollows of her throat.

"Let me come, make me come," she sobbed, shuddering under their ministrations. Again they both pulled back from her, and she screamed with thwarted need.

"We'll let you come in a minute," Alex said, happily, though his own voice was a little unsteady. "Just you tell us where Stephanie is, and we'll do it for you."

Poppy groaned, arching her back, tears in her eyes. She thought again of her mantra, her talisman phrase - honourable compromise - and wondered if she had fought hard enough for her pride. Her cunt was so swollen, so congested and juicy that she felt like a ripe fruit, ready to burst, and she didn't see how she could hold out any longer and keep her sanity.

"She's with the Tanners!" she shouted, but they both

looked blank, and neither one moved to give her what she craved.

"The bike gang - she's staying with them, out in the country - I'll take you to her, I'll take you there, now for Christ's sake get me off!" The last sentence was one desperate shriek of insatiable need, and she wondered what she would do if they didn't want to finish her after all.

"Good girl," Alex said, very kindly. "Will you do the business for her, Paul?"

"By all means," the sweetly sinful blond replied, lying down again and running his hand over her trembling, tormented body. He cupped his hand over her vulva and eased two fingers into her, thrusting more forcefully as he felt her eager, flooding wetness. Alex put his own hand on her mound and, with maddening slowness, stroked her clit with his thumb, rubbing softly in tight little circles. Poppy howled and came, thighs plunging, breasts heaving, thrashing so wildly that one of Paul's knot's came undone.

They held her until she was spent, kissing her face and forehead, cuddling her gently back down to earth as they untied her.

"It's two whole weeks," she said, with a sudden, beatific smile. "It's definitely time to go home. But first I'll take you to Stephanie."

TEN: The Last Day

The sun blazed down, turning the branches of the trees into shrivelling shadow-makers, casting an odd, almost static tracery over the naked bodies sprawled in the parched, bent grass. Stephanie lay replete between Rocky, who had just come long squirts of salty semen down her throat, and Budgie, whose cock had been buried deep in her pussy up until a couple of minutes ago. Her bottom was still rather sore, but the ache felt good rather than nasty, a well-earned, satisfying tenderness, like that of thoroughly-exercised muscles, a pleasant reminder of a challenge met. Currently she was basking in a post-orgasmic near dream state, though vaguely aware at the back of her mind that she ought to move soon, get further out of the midday sun. A case of raging sunburn would hardly be the best way to round off this adventure of hers, and rounding it off, she knew, was what she now planned to do. Shortly after waking, waking alone and well rested in the bunkhouse, it had occurred to her that she had now spent two whole eeks, or very nearly, at Tanners, and it really was time to think about going home.

This was nothing like her panic of the day before, no frantic urge for flight, more a remembrance that she did, after all, have responsibilities outside this woodland hide-away. One of them, in a way, was Poppy Ryanson, the reason for this escapade. Stephanie realised that she didn't even know if the little minx had made it to her flat, or had simply run off again - gone elsewhere. She told

155

herself that to doubt Poppy was all right was not only silly, but unnecessary; though they had only met once, she had felt such a strong bond between them that she was sure she would feel it, sense it, if Poppy was in any real trouble. More prosaically, Budgie, who was obviously very close to the little imp, would have surely mentioned something if there was anything to worry about. Well, anyway, wherever the other girl was, she must be thinking about returning home soon as well.

Having showered and put on Poppy's blue dress, the only thing she felt she could, in conscience, depart in, she had wandered through the encampment, acknowledging the waves and smiles on all sides, aware that she was liked and admired for having taken a hard punishment so stylishly, aware too that, if she wanted to, she could belong here now. Perhaps it was strange that the time felt right to leave now, just at the point of acceptance, but it also seemed perfectly appropriate; she no longer had anything to prove, there was no sense of running away, nothing left uncompleted. She had experienced this new environment in every aspect, but now she wanted her own life, her own home, her own friends.

She missed Alex and Paul, missed them suddenly and acutely, and wondered if they'd been missing her. She kept an image of them in her head as she went in search of Rocky, understanding in a way she hadn't understood before that, although Budgie was the one who had brought her here, Rocky was the one she ought to apply to first, for permission to depart in peace. The permission, she knew instinctively, would be given now, after the events of the previous night, as equally as permission to remain would be given should she ask; she had earned the right to go or stay, as she chose. She smiled wryly to herself, aware that some would find such conclusions absurd; there had never really been any sense that she was a captive, imprisoned here against her will, yet the way life was lived at Tanners seemed to demand certain conventions, certain unwritten rules that were necessary to sustain the unreal reality for those who lived there, and Stephanie, a creator of dreams herself, had never been fond of damaging or dismissing the dreams of others.

She had found Rocky talking to Budgie, the pair of them sitting under a tree quite near the road that ringed the whole site, discussing something intently, and she had wondered for a moment if she herself was the subject of discussion, especially as the whole tone of their conversation seemed to change when she approached them. Still, they invited her to sit down, and what had been a light-hearted exchange swiftly became a more ribald one.

Rocky was the first to suggest that she should present her beaten bottom for inspection, but Budgie was equally enthusiastic as she lifted up her skirt and demonstrated those marks and discolourations which lingered. A little judicious exploring of these honourable decorations soon began to make Stephanie's juices flow, and she shut her eyes and smiled as pleasure-pulses and little advance shocks raced along every nerve channel and energy current she possessed. Boldly, she initiated the next stage, stripping off her dress and suggesting to the men that they themselves might be cooler wearing less, an idea which was well received and promptly acted upon. The next step, quite naturally, was for Stephanie to crouch on all fours and take Rocky in her mouth while Budgie slipped easily into her hot, oily quim from behind, carefully avoiding too much pressure on the more tender areas of her rear, but paying plenty of attention to her clitoris, making her come at least twice in lovely, slow, overlapping spasms before she was satisfactorily filled at both ends.

Now, lying dreamily between them, Budgie stroking her hair at intervals, Rocky occasionally pinching one nipple, she let her sated mind work on the best way to introduce the subject of her return to the world outside.

The white Lotus, top down, gleamed in the blazing sunshine as it nosed into the traffic on the northbound bypass. Max, a pair of sunglasses and a black silk shirt giving him something of a Mafioso appearance, slotted a tape into the stereo and the hot, heavy air was suddenly full of the Ride of the Valkyries. Before she left, looking a little less pristine than she had on arriving, Miss Hughes had given him precise directions to the Tanners place, and her home telephone number. The former were in his wallet, the latter in a desk drawer for future consideration, as his most pressing and present concern was getting to Tanners and retrieving his wife.

He did wonder how the motorcycle gang would react when he arrived on their property and demanded Poppy's return. He did not think they would be too appalled at the prospect of parting with her - given the attractive investigator's account of the punishment Poppy had earned herself the previous night, his red-headed witch was undoubtedly making her presence felt amongst them. What had she done this time? Starting fights, provoking other girls, damaging property? He winced, a shade theatrically, wondering if he might find himself obliged to pay replacement costs for one or more motorbikes she had wrecked, or windows she had smashed.

Max knew he was being a little hard on his adored and adorable wife, whose sporadic vandalism was generally petty. But there had been an occasion at an admittedly unpleasant dinner party, where the hostess had not missed a single opportunity to insult poor Poppy in a variety of icily subtle but poisonous ways ... this had ultimately necessitated the purchase of an entire Royal Doulton dinner service to smooth things over, as it had been impossible to match two broken bowls, one shattered plate and a gravy boat.

Poppy, of course, had not realised at the time that some pieces of crockery were considerably more expensive than others, and had been genuinely contrite when he made the financial consequences of that particular tantrum clear to her, which had somewhat tested his ingenuity when it came to agreeing an appropriate punishment. He knew of one couple with a relationship similar to that within his own marriage, who had settled the matter of a badly-dented brand new car by the burning of a new and expensive dress, but he found that type of thing pointless and distasteful, and had instead given Poppy two hundred strokes of the heaviest cane, twenty a day and nothing less, until the sentence was completed.

The traffic was thinning out now, and he turned the music up as he increased his speed, contemplating various possible penalties his wife might deserve - indeed, require - for this wanton, unauthorised absence. His penis hardened appreciably as he put his foot on the accelerator, and he half-smiled.

Only now was he able to look back on the past fortnight with any clarity. It had been an odd mixture, a positive maelstrom of emotions. His initial reaction on finding the note had been rage, followed swiftly by a spell of acceptance; she would either reappear, head hanging, within hours, or telephone from somewhere, anxious to be extricated from some precarious situation or other. After forty-eight hours, though, he had been obliged to realise that this time Poppy had either made sensible and secret preparations for her escapade, or had been particularly lucky. Very well then, he had thought, let her have her fun - it would do her no harm to spend some time outside his protection. After all, her likeliest whereabouts were somewhere in the vicinity of Budgie Barr, who knew her ways and was fond enough of her to ensure that she came to no harm. Tracking her down immediately and dragging her home might not give her the chance to appreciate what she had left behind - and as for the new Porsche he had promised her, well, he had contemplated buying one for her birthday anyway. The bet was nothing - what counted was the fact that his wife was satisfied.

Receiving the e-mail had spurred him into action for two conflicting reasons; the main one being what was not said in the short message she had sent. Max knew his wife well enough to read between the lines; despite the gloating bravado, underneath was slightly resentful bewilderment that he had not yet tracked her down. The other factor in his decision to contact a detective agency was the sheer surprise of receiving e-mail from his wife. He had assumed she was with Budgie Barr, yet would the primitive, communal lifestyle he had heard Barr lived lend itself to electronic communications? Now, however, Miss Hughes had confirmed that Poppy was indeed at this Tanners place, and he had immediately set off to collect her. However, as he approached the junction at which he had been directed to turn off the motorway, he experienced a worrying flash of doubt. Computers with Net access in some hooligans' holiday camp seemed less than plausible - less plausible than the possibility that Miss Hughes had made a mistake. Reaching out, he switched off the music in an attempt to collect his thoughts.

The solution, which came to him almost instantly, was so simple as to be absurd. Poppy was not, after all, a prisoner of these people, nor were they entirely barbarian savages just because they had different priorities. If his wife had wanted to send an e-mail, she would have asked Barr or one of his friends to take her to the nearest bar or cafe offering communication facilities to customers - including anonymous mailing. He smiled, the heart-stopping lurch of fear dissipating as though it had never occurred.

As Max negotiated the narrower roads, forcing himself to keep the Lotus at a reasonably safe speed, he felt his erection growing again as he mentally listed the ways in which he could teach his errant wife the lesson she would want and need. There was, after all, the delicate and endlessly fascinating balance of their relationship to protect and even strengthen. Well, he could whip her, or cane her, or restrain her. He could tie her up and refrain from beating her. He could chastise her without letting her climax for a set period of time. He could oblige her to bring herself to orgasm without allowing her access to his own body ... there were so many subtle and unsubtle ways to reinforce the bond between them, and all that really mattered was to find the way that gave the maximum mutual satisfaction.

There was a junction coming up. He pulled into the side of the road for a moment to consult the directions Miss Hughes had given him. While he was making sure of his route, he heard the throaty, thundering growl of a motor-cycle engine and, shortly afterwards, a powerful bike shot past him, the pillion passenger wearing barely-decent denim shorts and a brief, cutaway t-shirt of shocking pink silk. He drew in breath a little quickly, turning to stare after the speeding machine and breathing out in a harsh sigh when he saw that the girl had very dark, almost black hair billowing freely from beneath her crash helmet. He turned the key in the ignition and set off again, aware that he was now very close to his goal.

The fields on either side of the road looked tired and somehow subjugated after more than a week without a drop of rain, and he wondered just how much of a fire-risk this area was. At least Poppy had never shown any

161

propensity for arson as a way of getting attention.

Round the next bend he caught sight of the sign Miss Hughes had described and, though the road was narrow, he stopped the car again and got out to look at it for himself.

The artwork was amateurish, but had a certain raw power to it; a very convincing sense that the artist knew exactly how it felt to apply hand or implement to insolently pert and jiggling buttocks made Max smile, made the hairs on the back of his neck stand up briefly with a wave of profound desire. Soon now, so very soon, his wife would be in his possession again, squirming in his arms, sobbing with bliss under the lash. His penis throbbed almost painfully and Max, normally the most controlled of men, did something he would never have imagined himself doing on an open road in broad daylight. He unfastened his expensive trousers, took out his hot, engorged, aching member and began to stroke it, gripping the swollen stem, sliding his hand up and down it, hard and fast, his breath coming in short gasps. In his mind's eye, Poppy was bound and helpless in front of him, begging for his seed, begging him to spurt it over her marked and mottled backside. With a hoarse grunt of determination he clutched himself, jerked his hips forward and ejaculated pearly strings of white into the dusty grass at the foot of the sign.

Poppy had held them up for about half an hour assembling the various clothes and shoes that were definitely hers, but at least it had given Paul the opportunity to consider that Stephanie might also require a change of clothes. He had found a simple white cotton sundress that Poppy had clearly spurned as too ordinary, hanging at the back of the wardrobe, and carried it out to Alex's Granada along with Poppy's assorted plastic bags. The girl had a wild, perverse, compelling charm about her, Paul reflected, and it was becoming easier to understand that she'd all but bewitched Stephanie into trading places with her and venturing off into the complete unknown. Poppy also, quite brazenly, took responsibility for the distress he and Alex had suffered, explaining that Steph had wanted them to be told of her whereabouts, but she herself had neglected to do anything about it. Paul's relief at discovering that Steph had neither forgotten nor deliberately abandoned him made it much easier for him to forgive the mercurial red-headed trigger of the whole situation.

Alex, too, was in far higher spirits than he had been an hour ago, and when they were finally in the car and on their way, he turned the radio up as loud as it would go and sang lustily along to the Saturday Rock Show.

Poppy had insisted on sitting next to him so she could give him directions, and he had no problem with that; she was a sexy little piece and no mistake. He thought back to their session in Stephanie's bedroom - what a lovely snatch the girl had, all wet and welcoming. It might have been fun simply to get stuck in, get on top and take her while she was tied to the bed - she would have loved it too. Still, pleasure was pleasure and there might be another opportunity. Anyway, though the attraction was sweet and strong, it didn't really hold up in comparison with the prospect of getting his hands, not to mention mouth and everything else, on Stephanie once again. He raised an ironic eyebrow as he drove down the slip road and on to the motorway.

The traffic was reasonably light, and he relaxed into his driving, turning the stereo down lightly in deference to his passengers. He had covered another six or seven miles when he felt the firm pressure of her hot little hand on his knee.

"Cut that out," he said, not looking at her, and heard her giggle. Was she reading his thoughts? Probably not, probably just felt like a bit of fun. Spontaneity was a quality he liked in a woman, but spontaneity at seventy or eighty miles an hour was just possibly pushing one's luck a little. He kept his eyes on the road, listening to the rustle and fumble next to him, and then the hand was back, touching the top of his thigh, moving upwards and inwards to his groin, one teasing finger tracing the outline of his cock, which rapidly unfurled and stiffened.

"Pack it up," he said, beginning to feel alarmed, but the mischievous hand had found his zip and was slowly and determinedly tugging it down. He tightened his grip on the wheel and swallowed hard, his pulse racing. It had been a fantasy of his in the past, sure, the blow-job at the wheel, but when a man drove for a living, he knew the risks ... What the hell was she going to do? Was she really going to go for it? He risked a sideways glance and saw she was leaning over, very slowly, lowering her head as she undid his flies, all the way, fumbling for his now hard cock, which sprang out through the opening in his clothes. Alex was in a quandary - he had told her to pack it up and she wouldn't, and there was no way of slowing down or pulling over, nowhere to stop, at least for the moment. Oh, the hell with it, if it was that inevitable, he'd better just cross his fingers and pray to the decanonised St Christopher not to pile the lot of them into the central reservation. He bit his lip, and tried to concentrate on driving as her soft, wet, warm mouth closed affectionately over his erection and her tongue began to swirl around his cockhead, licking and teasing and pleasing. He clung to the wheel, eyes wide, the fear he felt blending with and heightening the intense physical pleasure of her expert fellation, his mind filling with a crazy, dangerous exhilaration. Oh God, she was rubbing his balls as well, stroking

164

the skin of his sacs, and her little tongue kept twizzling and twirling as she sucked and sucked, steady and greedy and unstoppable. Somehow he kept his feet on the pedals and his eyes open while the utterly superlative, terrifying roller-coaster sensations built up and up and up inside him, until he couldn't hold it back any longer and spurted uncontrollably, letting out a shout of relief as he shot his seed down her throat.

The car swerved a little, but he corrected and straightened the wheel, just as he caught sight of an upcoming lay-by. Poppy sat up, giggling and unrepentant as he swung the Granada off the road and parked, switching off the engine and gasping for breath. He couldn't claim he hadn't enjoyed it, but at the same time, she really needed to learn a lesson about road safety. Well, he'd just have to apply one.

"All right?" Paul asked, sounding more amused than bothered. Alex shook his head, not in negation but more as a reflex, and flung open the door on his side.

"Get out of the car, you silly bitch," he snapped at Poppy, who sniggered, then looked sulky.

"What's the matter, didn't you like it? You seemed to," she pouted, and licked her lips ostentatiously. Alex jumped out of the car, marched round the front of it, yanked open the passenger door and hauled her unceremoniously out onto the verge. Paul opened the rear door, suddenly less amused.

"Don't chuck her out, we don't know where we're going."

"I'm not going to chuck her out," Alex retorted, and when Paul still looked worried, winked at him, unseen by Poppy who wailed in protest. He shoved her over the bonnet of the car, snatched her skirt up and gave her eight hard smacks on her bare bottom, which she received with loud and unconvincing yells. Picking her up by the scruff of her neck, he turned her back towards the car.

"If you ever, *ever* pull a stunt like that again ..." he snapped, and Poppy started to say something, but shut up as she caught sight of his expression. Alex, no longer really angry, if he had ever been at all, half-laughed as he finished his sentence. "Just you make sure you do it with a bloody good driver."

He thrust her into Paul's arms, as the latter leaned out to receive her.

"You can mind her the rest of the way," he said, laughing genuinely now. "Have fun with her yourself if you like, just keep her out of my hair."

Paul, grinning widely, pulled Poppy into the back seat, laying her across his lap and administering a few slaps himself as Alex restarted the car.

"If I promise to behave, can I sit up?" Poppy demanded, a couple of miles further on. Paul acquiesced and let her arrange herself on the seat beside him and smooth her tangled hair. Both of these men had quite hard hands, she thought, shifting her rear against the warm leather seat, but Paul had placed the spanks more precisely and knowledgeably than Alex, for all the dark-haired driver's calculated air of seductive menace. If anything, she suspected that Paul might be the more masterful between the sheets, and wondered how much of a likelihood there was of ever finding out if she was right. Probably little or none unless she took her chances right now, she decided, and slipped the straps of her dress off her shoulders, tapping Paul on the arm to attract his attention. He smiled happily as he turned and saw her naked breasts, the nipples hard with excitement, and he reached out, taking firm hold of each tit, squeezing experimentally then drawing back and pinching the nipples, pulling them so she growled huskily and thrust her chest further forward, arching her neck and putting her arms behind her back.

"Come on, play with me," she whispered, and Paul clearly had no objection to indulging her.

"I thought she was supposed to be behaving herself," Alex, who must have glimpsed her in the rear view mirror, remarked, but Paul just laughed.

"I can handle her. You just get on with the driving," he said. Alex, with an exaggerated shrug, did precisely that while Paul leaned over and took Poppy's right breast in his mouth, using his teeth to apply an ecstasy-generating sharp pressure that made the juices flow and bubble in her hot quim. He bit her other breast as well, and when he moved his head from one to the other she could see the marks of his teeth, little red and white lines around each nipple. He pushed her breasts together and did his best to get both nipples into his mouth at once, sucking and biting and nibbling with expertise and obvious enjoyment.

Poppy leaned back a little, closing her eyes and surrendering herself to the sensations, clenching her thigh muscles as the pressure built inside her.

Paul stopped chewing on her breasts and began to slap then lightly, making them flush red all over and jiggle, the heavy softness wobbling from side to side under the rain of smacks, making her moan deep in her throat. If this car ride was the last of her freedom, she was certainly getting the most she could out of it in terms of memories to carry away with her ... and stories to drive her darling husband wild with lechery and delight.

"You going to fuck her?" Alex asked, half-turning his head to leer at the pair of them.

"I might," Paul said, distractedly, more interested in Poppy's boobs than in continuing the conversation. He didn't think it would be either easy or comfortable to attempt full penetration on the back seat of a speeding car, but his cock was hard, his blood up, and he knew plenty of other ways to obtain mutual gratification.

"I get the feeling you like to use your mouth," he said to Poppy, who formed her lips into a circle and blew him a kiss.

"Come on then, show *me* what you can do with that wicked mouth of yours. If you did it for him, you can do it for me too. Show me how good you are with it."

She wriggled right out of her dress as she got up, twisting round to kneel on the seat beside him, crouching over him and pulling down the zip of his trousers with her teeth, a refinement which was exciting but slightly unnerving, and he felt himself wilting a little, but the scent of her, the scent of female heat, soon put him right again, pervading his senses and quickening his loins.

More than ready now, he helped her by lifting his hips and pushing down the waistband of trousers and pants, giving her room to do it all properly.

She started off by lapping the head of his cock, the little jabbing movements of her tongue making it bob in his lap. Then she took hold of his shaft with her slender hand and gripped him firmly while her tongue rotated around his glans, all over the head of it and along the slit, around and around, moving on to lick up and down the shaft, her tongue warm and silky, her fingers smooth and cool.

He groaned, and she paused for a second, then opened her mouth wide and engulfed him with measured, mind-bending slowness, taking every inch of him, setting up a powerful rhythmic suction on his straining cock, hot juicy mouth enclosing him, saliva trickling onto his balls, soft friction of her tongue, and he twisted his fingers in her hair and whispered hoarsely, "Yeah, oh yeah ..." as she sucked and sucked until he couldn't resist her any longer and came deeply and thoroughly in her mouth.

When he was empty, she let his cock slide out between her lips, but lingered in position, resting her head in his lap, cheek against his belly, breathing heavily as he stroked her back, sweeping his hand down to the curve of her arse, which was still a little red from their earlier onslaught, and warmer to his questing hand than the rest of her body.

He stroked the cheeks he had previously smacked, feeling his way under the swell and probing for her pussy, which was wet again, puffy and juicy, and he began to frig her, reaching round to tug sharply on her nipples as his fingers worked busily in her dripping cleft, and she bucked and squealed, orgasming almost instantly with a gush of juices over his burrowing hand ...

"Anyone need a drink?" Alex asked suddenly. "Only there's a service station coming up, and I could do with a Coke or something."

"Wouldn't mind one myself," Paul said. "Oh, by the way Poppy, are we going to be leaving you at this place when we pick Steph up, or what?"

Alex chuckled. "Sounds like she'd be right at home there. Still, what do you want us to do with you, babe? We can drop you off somewhere, or take you home if you want."

Poppy was wriggling back into the grey flowered dress, which was now looking distinctly crumpled.

"Oh, I'll get Max to come and pick me up - my husband," she said. "It won't take him long to get there. Actually, if we're stopping, I can phone him now." She let out a naughty giggle. "That ought to give him something to think about - if I just tell him where to meet me ..."

She was feeling highly exhilarated, beaming with happiness, greater happiness than could be ascribed to the after-effects of orgasm alone. She was going home! She was going home, with her head held high, all doubts and fears discarded. She could hardly wait to reach a phone, to hear her husband's voice again, to speak to him, to tell him everything, and place herself back in his possession, back where she really belonged.

ELEVEN: Come Together

There was a point where the road petered out into the kind of gravel track that Max was reluctant to take the Lotus any further along, fearing for his paintwork as well as his suspension. Still, the grassy ground on either side was flat enough and dry enough to park without having to worry about being bogged down - not that this was likely, given the long, hot, dry August. Picking up his jacket, which he carried more as a repository for wallet, phone and keys than for warmth, he locked the car and continued on foot, seeing the crossing which Miss Hughes had described as a ring road of sorts, around the heart of the Tanners stronghold. Over to the north, the sky was beginning to darken, the sunlight to take on a metallic, brassy note, and he hoped he could collect his wife and get away with reasonable speed. Deciding to approach with a degree of caution, he turned to the left and followed the route into the trees. If luck was with him, he might even be able to find Poppy alone, and simply take her away.

After approximately ten minutes of measured walking he heard voices, male and female, talking and laughing, so he left the track and began to make his way through the trees, moving carefully, trying not to fall over anything or tear his clothes on stray branches. He still considered himself as fully in control, but perhaps his earlier, almost territorial spell of masturbation at the entrance to this place had combined with his acute longing for his wife to override his normal self-discipline, because when he saw the rear view of a red-haired girl, a curvy, beautiful redhead, just getting to her feet as she said something to one of her two companions, he simply rushed out into the open and shouted her name at the full pitch of his lungs.

It seemed like an endless, frozen second of seeing everything at once; registering the chunky, shaven-headed figure of Budgie Barr as well as another, very large and aggressive looking male, the girl turning round with a hand to her mouth and a shocked look in her eyes; realising it wasn't Poppy, wasn't her at all, and the great braying shout of laughter from Barr that made him want to knock the stupid oaf senseless. Almost robbed of his breath, Max stopped, stumbled, and bent over, grasping his thighs, mouth hanging open, slowly shaking his head from side to side in shock and denial. It wasn't Poppy, this pretty redhead with Budgie Barr. It was some other red-haired girl - so where was his wife? Where was she?!

Stephanie nearly jumped out of her skin when she heard someone shouting Poppy's name. As the man came running out of the trees and Budgie started to roar with laughter, she put two and two together and decided that this had to be Poppy's husband, finally arriving at Tanners to look for his wife. The man looked like he'd been kicked in the head when she turned round and let him see her face, see who she was and, apart from Budgie's cackles of laughter, there was no sound from anyone.

Rocky, showing the most presence of mind, calmly put his trousers back on, somehow managing to invest the procedure with a degree of dignity. Having buttoned up his flies, he elbowed Budgie in the ribs, and the younger biker swiftly followed suit, even though he was still snorting with laughter.

Steph herself made no move to grab her dress, not particularly bothered that this man could see her naked

172

body. Her body was nothing to be ashamed of, and more than enough people had seen it, both last night and over the preceding couple of weeks. Poppy's husband was not, at present, displaying any great awareness that she stood nude in front of him. He had dropped wordlessly onto the grass, and was sitting with his head in his hands, obviously incapable of saying anything at all, and probably wishing the ground would open and swallow him up alive. Feeling sorry for him, Steph went up close and touched his shoulder, almost shyly.

"Mr ... uh, Ryanson?"

"How the hell do you know my name?" he snarled, whipping upright so fast that Stephanie jumped back and nearly fell over. Rocky was instantly beside her, looking every bit as formidable as he had to Stephanie on her first morning.

"Don't get over-excited, there," he said, and the man looked him up and down and made a visible effort to keep his temper under control.

"I'm ... sorry to trespass," he said, quietly. "I'm looking for my wife. I was told she was here. Her name is Poppy Ryanson."

"She ain't here," Budgie said, gleefully. "She's fooled you good and proper this time, hasn't she?"

Seeing the danger-lights in his eyes, Stephanie quickly stepped in between him and Budgie before either one could actually get as far as throwing a punch.

"She's perfectly all right," she said quickly, and when he looked at her in what seemed like disbelief, felt an odd tremble run through her body - a curious sense of shifting. Her last sentence had been polite, placating, deferential, and she had been putting as much girly femininity into it as possible, but something about this man's demeanour had roused her other self, her old self with a new addition and, despite her nakedness and her recently-beaten bottom, it was Madame Stephanie now, Madame Stephanie confronting this slight, sophisticated, and potentially dangerous man.

"I know exactly where your wife is, Mr Ryanson. She's in my flat. We swapped lives for a bit. If you'd care to drive me home, you can collect her at the same time."

The man stroked his chin, but there was something of respect in his attitude now; not subservience, but the courtesy awarded to a peer.

"I see. I understand, or I believe I am beginning to. You are here on some kind of exchange visit, while my wife is living in your home. Yes, I believe I understand."

"More than I fucking do!" Rocky interrupted. He turned to Budgie, who had finally composed himself and was standing quietly by. "You in on this too, you shitehawk?" Budgie's lips twitched again, but he nodded, and Rocky hooked his thumbs into his belt loops and looked from one to another, from Budgie to Stephanie then back to the newcomer.

"Taking one bird instead of another, messing about all over the shop, telling lies," he grumbled into his beard. "I don't know …" Quite suddenly he laughed, a deep belly laugh, and held out one huge hand to Poppy's husband.

"Bloody women, eh? Nothing but trouble." He turned to Stephanie again. "And you're not even the usual sort of girl, are you? You're one of the other sort. Well, you've done your mate proud, haven't you? Good on you." He hugged her roughly, lifting her off her feet, then depositing her in front of the small, slim man. "Guess you'd better take this one with you if she wants to go. Just you …" pinching Stephanie's bottom, "you come back and see us again. And bring this mate of yours with you, and all."

Budgie rolled his eyes. "She's even more trouble than this one, Rocky," he objected. "And she's been bad enough." He turned Steph round to face him and kissed her mouth.

"You're all right, though. You stood up to us fine. Like Rocky says, come back again some time."

This was the precise moment at which a loud, high-pitched trill sounded, and Poppy's husband snatched a small mobile phone out of his jacket pocket and put it to his ear. As he took the call, a huge variety of expressions washed over his face - shock, triumph, amusement, astonishment and delight.

"Yes," he said at first, then: "Indeed. And where - ?" He held up one hand to Stephanie and the bikers, indicating that they should keep quiet as he continued to speak. "I see," he murmured, nodding his head. "At the Blue ... and then, yes, all right. Very well. I shall. I am. Goodbye." He snapped the phone's mouthpiece shut and returned it to his pocket, smiling in a particularly satisfied manner.

"That," he said calmly, "was my wife. She is at present on her way here, in a car with someone - I have no idea who. But she is coming here, and wishes me to drive over here and collect her. I didn't tell her that I have already arrived, because it occurred to me that some form of welcome ceremony might be appropriate, as I think Poppy has put every one of us to a great deal of trouble. Do you think something of the sort could be arranged?"

"A nice smacked bum, maybe?" Budgie suggested. "We do 'em in bulk here, you know." Poppy's husband seemed to be thinking it over, and his eyes kept returning to Stephanie, who was wishing and almost hoping that he would give her the opportunity, or at least let her watch Little Trouble get her just deserts. Their eyes met again, and again that feeling of mutual respect, of shared ideology, passed between them.

"You, more than the rest of us, have been inconvenienced by Poppy," he said. "If you yourself would like to see that she makes amends, then I would be more than willing to permit you."

"I wouldn't mind seeing that," Budgie said lasciviously. Rocky shot him a look of only-half-humourous warning, but Mr Ryanson didn't seem to be offended.

"I have no objection to all of you watching, if you wish. It might be as well to settle the matter before I take my wife away."

Rocky looked pleased. "A show's a show, and I reckon this girl here will give us all a good one - won't you, darling?" He ruffled Stephanie's hair and she felt herself blush slightly - she wasn't, perhaps, entirely back to her former self yet, but the idea of punishing Poppy again, getting another crack - quite literally - at that gloriously responsive little bum, was making her insides quiver with delight. Poppy's husband held out his hand to her, with an odd but touching formality.

"My name is Max Ryanson, and I would be happy for you to … chastise my wife," he said.

Stephanie took the proffered hand, which was slender but very strong, and smiled at him. "Stephanie Ames, and it would be my pleasure," she replied.

Though she hadn't let Alex or Paul see it, or at least hoped she hadn't, Poppy had been slightly worried that she might have trouble with the final stages of finding the way to the Tanners place. She had not, after all, ever been there herself, but Budgie had told her where it was, and even shown her some photographs. Still, seeing the sign and the turning that would take them right into the enclave, she felt a definite relief, and even laughed when she noticed how both the men goggled at the painted sign when they passed it.

"This is interesting," Alex murmured as the Granada bounced and banged down the road. "Anyone else seen

Deliverance?"

Paul, clinging on to the door handle with one hand and Poppy with the other, didn't answer. Poppy, hanging halfway out of the window, shaded her eyes with her hand and let out a whoop. "There's someone there, by the trees! Here, pull over!" When Alex obliged, she got the door open and slipped smartly out of Paul's hold, bolting off down the track at a speed that was frankly inadvisable in the flimsy silver sandals she still wore.

Stephanie, waiting patiently in the heat, was disconcerted when she saw the car come down the track, as it looked curiously familiar. In fact, it looked a lot like Alex McCoy's Granada, but it couldn't be, surely. Still, this was definitely Poppy Ryanson, coming at her like a bat out of hell. She took a deep breath and stepped forward, still naked apart from her red cowboy boots; she had put her dress back on but, sticky with the now-oppressive heat, had taken it off again. What the hell.

"Poppy," she said, and Poppy halted her headlong run, looked at her, then flung her arms round Stephanie's neck.

"Hello! Hello! Have you had a good time? I have, and I've come to send you home - unless you want to stay here, of course!" she finished with a naughty giggle. Disengaging herself, she took in Stephanie's nakedness and giggled again.

"Wouldn't they let you have any clothes?"

"Clothes? Who needs them?" Stephanie asked rhetorically, and grabbed the shoulder straps of Poppy's filmy dress, yanking them down so the dress fell right off Poppy's pretty body.

"Naughty girls like you don't need clothes, anyway. Not for what you're about to get."

She had been too intent on Poppy to notice that the car's

driver and another passenger had also got out and were approaching, but hearing Alex's voice right by her ear was almost enough to strike her speechless.

"Whatever you're going to do to her, she probably deserves it," he said, and Stephanie looked at him and Paul in incredulous delight.

"What's this - a class reunion?" she asked shakily. She wanted to grab the pair of them, smother them with kisses and shag them both senseless, but there was the small matter of Poppy's punishment to take care of first. Poppy, however, took advantage of her momentary distraction and turned to run.

"Can't catch me!" she yelled, feinting left and darting to the right.

"Want to bet?" Paul said sweetly, seizing her arm and whirling her back. "What are you going to do with her, Stephanie?"

Stephanie stretched, catlike, flexing her fingers, feeling the crackle of her muscles, her body coming alive to full awareness, eager anticipation.

"Oh, I have a little something planned for her. I'm sure you two will enjoy it as well. Why don't you help me get her down there?"

Poppy wailed, and tried to kick Paul in the shins, but Alex, having snatched up her discarded dress and tucked it into his belt, got behind her and took hold of her shoulders, lifting her up so Paul could grab her lower legs and take her off the ground completely. With Stephanie leading the way, they went down the slope and into the main courtyard, where the whipping block from the previous night had been set up in the centre of a ring of parked motorbikes, and the box of whips, canes and other necessities was sitting beside it. Poppy stopped yelling when she saw this significant still life, and a wide, wanton smile appeared on her face.

"It's all right, they're friends of mine," Stephanie announced, indicating Alex and Paul as Budgie, Rocky, Patch and everyone else emerged from the bunkhouses and formed a larger ring outside the courtyard. The door to Rocky's own, smaller building was left ajar, with those between it and the whipping block standing far enough apart to allow an uninterrupted line of sight, and Steph sent a nod of recognition in that direction before taking a grip of Poppy's tousled red hair.

"You can put her down, I'll deal with her," she said, and the two men obeyed, retreating to the circle of watchers, who calmly made room for them. Poppy didn't fight as Steph led her to the block, bent her over it and began to bind her to it, hand and foot, using the hanks of soft, black rope she had found in the box. She had always been justifiably proud of her knots, and took this opportunity to demonstrate her skill. The light seemed to be changing a little, and when she looked up at the sky, she saw it had grown darker, with massing clouds, but as yet it seemed only to be adding a certain ambience to the afternoon, rather than posing a threat of anything really untoward in the way of weather.

She contemplated Poppy's rump for a moment, noticing a pink tinge to the otherwise pearly whiteness of the girl's fair skin, and wondered just who had administered a spank or three to that gorgeous backside. It didn't matter: she was going to administer something more than that.

She stepped back for a moment, raised her hand, and let fly. Poppy squeaked, then fell silent, apart from the occasional gasp as Steph spanked her, full, open-handed, noisy smacks in a fast, determined rhythm, a flurry of blows that rapidly reddened that pert little bottom to a deep, heated blush. Only when her own hand was tingling and beginning to sting did she pause.

"Better?" she enquired solicitously as Poppy whim-

179

pered.

"A little," the other replied, and Stephanie bent over to pick up a fine, whippy, medium-weight cane from the box. She circled Poppy once, caressing her heated rear, massaging the glowing cheeks, tracking two fingers down the ridge of her spine, feeling the thin film of oily sweat on the girl's skin, the faint but perceptible trembling of her body, which was a reaction to the adrenaline coursing though her system. Poppy lifted her head to show a face almost as suffused with blood as her bottom, the pupils of her eyes dilated, and she gave an uncertain little grin.

Stephanie returned to her previous spot, just behind Poppy's raised, tensing buttocks, and laid down a single, beautifully placed stroke of the cane, as hard as she could. It bit smartly into Poppy's arse, and rebounded away to leave a white line that rapidly darkened, provoking a high-pitched yell from the tightly-bound victim, whose arms jerked in a vain and probably involuntary reflex; a command from mind to body to clutch and rub the injured part. Stephanie laid down three more strokes with practically no pauses in between, a rapid crack-crack-crack almost like gunfire, and rubbed the vivid marks herself, massaging Poppy with smooth, circular movements. The girl was hissing as she sucked in breath through her clenched teeth, and Stephanie tapped her bottom lightly with the cane.

"Quiet, aren't you?" she observed, and struck the crease between thigh and buttock with precise and deadly accuracy. A wail broke from Poppy's lips, and she began to fidget, bumcheeks clenching and unclenching, feet scrabbling fruitlessly in the dirt.

"Be still," Stephanie said pitilessly, and gave her the sixth one, slightly missing her intended placing, overlaying an earlier stroke but generating another loud howl from the bound girl.

"Stephanie - Madame, I need to pee, I think," Poppy gasped, trying to pull free of the ropes, which were too securely tied to give her any leeway.

"Tell someone who cares," Stephanie rejoined, returning her attention to the box of treats nearby. Her own blood was heating up, her vulva slick with moisture and her nipples standing proud. Perhaps she'd get the little bitch to lick her pussy out as well before she was done.

Everyone was still watching her in silence, and though she made no outward indication that she was even aware of their presence, she actually felt strengthened by it, borne up on a wave of admiration and shared sensuality, privileged and proud and more than ever determined to perform as properly as she ever had before she came here.

She found the paddle of polished wood, the one she was sure had been used on her, and considered applying this fearsome weapon to Poppy's now well-marked cheeks, but found, hefting it in her hand, that it was really too heavy for her to wield with comfort or, indeed, with real skill. She rummaged further and laid hands on another paddle, made of shiny black leather, three layers bound together and squared off at the end, with a rigid, wrapped handled, and settled on that as a good stinger if properly used.

Applied, it made a loud, crisp, smacking sound and she set to, paddling the girl vigorously, not bothering to count individual strokes, alternating from left to right buttock with elegant, percussive power. Poppy began to cry out as soon as the first blow landed, and kept up a medley of cries, moans and, as the paddling continued, sobs, but Stephanie felt no inclination to halt until the girl gave a long, howling moan and started pissing forcefully onto the dusty ground. Stephanie raised an eyebrow and stood back, wiping the sweat from her forehead and feeling her arm beginning to ache.

"I think she may have had enough, from me, anyway,"

she said, softly, then cleared her throat. "I'm done with her for now," she went on, loudly and clearly, aware that the words had an almost ritual weight, looking round the ring of faces and seeing, with a combination of relief and regret, that Max Ryanson had appeared, and was walking across the open space, at an angle such that it would be impossible for Poppy to see him, walking with slow, measured steps and a sardonic smile. It occurred to Stephanie that the distant rumble of thunder from the darkening clouds lent an even greater dramatic grandeur to that long, slow, beautiful moment when Max Ryanson came out into the heavy amber sunlight to reclaim his wife.

The ropes that held her wrists and ankles were skilfully tied, firm and constricting without being wretchedly so, and Poppy simply gave herself up to their power while Stephanie punished her. It felt so right, so darkly ecstatic, to be restrained like this, unable to move away, to wriggle or squirm or rub herself as her bottom was punished; the scattergun of a real hand-spanking, the cruel bite of the cane - *six* vicious ones, the bitch, and then that smarting little paddle, stinging and hurting, so hot and sharp she'd been unable to keep her bladder under control … And now there was this intermission, this calm, filled with a sense of voluptuous tension, a knowledge of something drawing near, something else, something all-consuming. Was Stephanie going to let the whole lot of them have a go at her now? What on earth would Max say if he arrived and found her like this, or impaled on someone's cock, or shrieking under someone else's whip or cane? Would he beat Stephanie for letting his wife be beaten so thoroughly? She almost began to laugh, but swallowed it down. Blood rushing to her head, everything dizzy, whirling gently around her. Thunder growled in the sky, like an angry deity, and she wondered for a moment if the power of her own imagination and desire had conjured him up for her. He couldn't possibly be here already yet, through the blurry sparkles before her eyes, she thought she could see Max. *Max!* He was there, crouching beside her, one hand on the nape of her neck, speaking her name!

She blinked away a mixture of sweat and tears and focused on him properly.

"Master," she whispered. "I've been a very bad girl, haven't I?"

He was stroking her hair, smiling rather than stern, but nonetheless she found herself beginning to cry again. He put a finger to her lips and shook his head.

"No more tears, now. Save them for later," he said softly, and started to untie her, slipping the knots free and unwinding the turns of the rope. Poppy was bewildered, almost afraid, as the ropes fell away and her husband pulled her to her feet. He had come out of nowhere, and though she was bound, he had untied her, and hadn't even slapped her backside. Was he going to reject her? She sniffled to herself, trembling as he held her, standing behind her with his hands resting lightly on her shoulders. The thunder sounded again and a shiver went from the crown of her head right the way down to her toes.

"I believe these people will keep you, Poppy," Max said, quite clearly. "You'd probably make a reasonable substitute for Stephanie Ames, and these people might well be able to teach you more about discipline. They might even be able to teach you something about your place in the world, and how to fit into it. You see, while Miss Ames has had an interesting ... exchange trip here, she intends to go back to her own home now, which means there is a vacancy for a girl in need of regular punishment right here."

Poppy couldn't speak, her throat had closed up. Max was going to leave her here, he didn't want her back. She shivered more violently, frantically wondering what to do, what to say that would convince him she had learned her lesson, and then he turned her slowly round to face him, and dropped his hands to his sides.

"Unless, that is, you feel you've had enough adventures for the time being," Max said, and through her distress Poppy noticed something which both shocked her and raised her frightened, failing spirits; Max was not as icily calm as he had originally sounded, and when he went on, there was a tiny but detectable tremor in his voice. She had never seen him like this, never really been aware of how much power she had over him by virtue of her submission.

"You can come home if you wish, Poppy. Do you want to be taken home?" he asked her, and Poppy burst into passionate tears, flinging herself down on her knees and hugging his legs, clutching him tightly, crying loudly and unrestrainedly.

"Take me home, Master, take me home!" she wept. "I'm sorry - I love you so much, please take me home."

"Get up, little slut," Max said kindly, and when she did, he moved with the swift strength that had often surprised those deceived by his slight build and soft speech. He pushed her up against the block she'd been tied to only minutes before and spread her legs, holding her in place with an iron grip of her left breast, digging his neat nails into the flesh, opening his trousers with the other hand and plunging himself forcefully inside her wet, swollen, juicy quim.

Max noted one split second of astonishment at himself, for the second time that afternoon. He was not unaccustomed to punishing his wife in front of other people, nor was it unheard of for him to delegate the act of beating her to someone else, but the most blatantly sexual elements of their relationship had always been kept for their times alone together. Now, though, he simply gave himself up to his overriding and irresistible impulse to fuck his wife hard, to reclaim her, to fill her, to possess her. Poppy had one foot on the floor, one hand clutching the whipping block in an effort to maintain her precarious balance, but her other arm was tightly round him as he pounded his cock into her, burying his face in the soft damp curve where her neck and shoulder joined, nipping at her skin, feeling her start to come, the tight pussy he so adored contracting round him, gloriously wet, dripping on his balls as she came. And he came too, tense shudders travelling all the way up and down his frame as the seed burst out of him and spurted into her obediently dilated and welcoming cunt.

He kept a firm hold of her as their breathing slowed at a matching pace, and then let her get her feet back on the ground, still resting his hand on her hip.

"If someone can provide you with something to wear, I'll take you home now, slut," he said, and Alex held out the crumpled grey dress.

"This is hers - and there's some other stuff in my car. If you walk up with me, I'll get it."

Max inclined his head, gracefully. "My thanks - to all of you."

"We've a dress in the car for you, too," Paul said to Stephanie as they waited for Alex to return. The Tanners had dispersed now, everyone pausing to give Steph a hug or kiss, with several invitations for her to come back another time, and bring her friends. Returning the hugs, Stephanie felt a little wistful, but happy in the knowledge that the invitations were sincere. She had proved herself, and shown them the other side of herself, and they accepted her as she was. Paul had said nothing as they walked towards the top of the slope, and when Alex's tall, slim figure came into view, his only comment was, "Come on then, here he is."

She walked on in silence, following Paul, her red boots, battered and dusty now, clumping on the hard ground. She felt strange, oddly flat, yet tense, almost on the verge of tears. What was Paul thinking? She didn't know how to ask him, and Alex, when they caught up with him, was equally blank faced, not really looking at her. They got to the car, and Stephanie stopped in her tracks, her eyes smarting.

"Are you all right?" Paul asked, and she shook her head.

"She is," she muttered, knowing they would understand who she meant.

"What's up, then?" Alex enquired, sounding more like his usual self.

"Will someone please - kiss me?" She was appalled by how wobbly and uncertain she sounded, but then Paul had wrapped his arms round her and was kissing her deeply and passionately, his tongue sliding into her mouth, his hands on her bare breasts, tender and sure. Alex joined the embrace, stroking her hair and planting a succession of kisses on her shoulders, and the sensitive spot at the back of her neck, lightly holding her waist. She broke the kiss with Paul, still stroking his face as she turned her head to kiss Alex, licking and nibbling at his lips and pushing her tongue between his teeth.

"You're all right, babe," Alex laughed as she turned back to Paul. "You're fine. You just need to come."

She looked from one to the other, aware again of the wet heaviness, the need between her legs, and nodded, remembering how many times she'd fantasised about having the two of them at once.

"Here? Now?" she asked, and Alex went to unlock the boot of the car.

"In a few seconds," he said, taking out an old, faded blanket and spreading it over the bonnet. "All right, Paul, let's get her up on here and do the business."

Stephanie was surprised but pleased at their assertiveness, and let them pick her up and arrange her on the bonnet of the car, her head pillowed on Alex's shoulder, her feet hanging apart over the radiator grille and her pussy exposed, open and wet. Alex kissed her face again, rubbing her nipples gently with his palm as Paul bent over her quim and began to kiss her there, licking her labia, pushing his fingers in and out of her hole, sucking her clit and using his hand to fuck her, licking determinedly while Alex held and kissed her, rolling her taut nipples between his index and middle fingers, whispering in her ear, "Go on baby, do it, come all over his face, come for us baby, you need it, you want it, come baby, come all over him, come on, baby, just come …"

Stephanie seemed to be cruising at the speed of light, on some perfect plateau of pleasure, warm waves of it rolling over and over her, thigh muscles jittering and spasming, toes curling in her boots, gasping and moaning aloud, held firmly and safely between her two lovers, held and teased and licked and sucked and stroked, and then the wave broke and she kicked and cried out, huge hard contractions in her womb and pussy, their hands tightening on her, holding her, making her come and come, thrashing there as the thunder roared above. Lightning flashes seared her eyes behind her squeezed-shut lids and finally, sweetly, deliciously cold and shocking, the rain began to fall on all three of them as she slowly shuddered to stillness.

TWELVE: Up where we Belong

·The curtains were open just enough to allow in the orangey-gold light of a full September moon, and on the bedside table were three glasses and a bottle of red wine.

Stephanie had put them there after dinner, but they had been so taken up with the three-way bondage game they were playing that they had not even opened the bottle and, although it was only ten past ten when they were satisfied with each other, all three had drifted off into a light post-coital doze. Waking again after about half an hour, Stephanie felt a familiar twinge in her vulva, the first faint stirrings of reviving desire. Cupping her left breast, she slid her other hand down between her legs, spreading the folds of flesh apart and exploring their moistening depths.

Though she was being careful, keeping her movements slight and slow, a clumsy shifting of her right elbow meant she brushed Paul's ribs and he, too, awoke.

"How you doing?" he murmured, and then his hand covered hers. "Still in the mood then? Well, well, well …"

Rolling over, he pressed himself against her and she could feel him hardening against her thigh. She curled her fingers around his shaft and began to slide them up and down, trailing her other hand across the chest of the still-sleeping Alex, bumping him with her left hip, licking one finger and touching his nipples until he opened his eyes and reached out for her, kissing her forehead, then the tip of her nose, working his way down to the hollow of her throat, down to her cleavage, licking the soft valley and nuzzling each breast. She stroked his hair and ran her nails down his back, and the three of them crushed together, hands touching and caressing.

They tended to arrange themselves for such encounters according to some almost telepathic communication pattern: there were rarely discussions or disagreements. This time, as Paul lay on his back, his cock rising up hard and proud, Steph crouched over him, facing his feet, and very slowly inserted him between her swollen, moist pussy lips. As she sank down on him, he ran his hands over her bottom and hips and reached round to fondle her clitoris, stimulating her as she gently drew him inside. Meanwhile Alex, at the end of the bed, could mould Steph's breasts in his hands, kneading the soft mounds as she bent further and further forward until his cock was just within reach of her mouth. She licked his glans then sucked him in, taking him deeply, sucking and salivating and lashing his shaft with her tongue.

He closed his eyes, sighing with enjoyment as she worked on him, allowing deep penetration of her mouth for a while and then easing him out, using her hands as her tongue circled the tip of his cock, treating it like an ice-cream cone, alternating firm pressure with lighter butterfly licks. She rubbed his balls with the very tips of her fingers, then moved her hands round to caress and squeeze his bottom, which was still tender from the earlier session, when she'd used the red rubber whip. The contrast between the former spanking, which inflamed the nerve-endings and stirred the senses one way, and this pure, unadulterated pleasure enhanced both for him, the memory and the present reality, and he tightened his grip on her breasts, pinching the nipples harder as her fingers were digging into his arse, soft strands of her hair falling down, brushing his balls and the tops of his thighs, and he began to breath more noisily, unable to keep back the little

murmurs and groans of pleasure, trying not to thrust too
hard into her mouth as the powerful tingling pressure
grew and grew, both in his balls and along the length of
his shaft, and he simply had to give in and climax, feeling
it break out of him, spurting and shooting, pulling back a
little so it went over her breasts and hair, as well as into
her mouth, and then feeling her gentle kisses on his thighs
as he subsided.

Having come himself, Alex now turned his attention to
working on Stephanie, who was already in the grip of
intense sexual arousal, her pussy clamping hard around
Paul's erection as the latter teased her with slow, erratic
movements, one hard, piercing thrust now and again, in
between spells of a gentler rocking motion, and a light,
constant, delicate circling of her clitoris. Alex's spunk
was all over her face and neck, and now he was holding
her upper body, twiddling her nipples, pulling them out
and pinching the very tips, kissing her and supporting her
as Paul drove into her from beneath, harder now, the
fingers against her clitoris working faster, more insistently, and she smiled to herself, her hands against Alex's
chest, kissing him and nibbling him, shoulders, nipples,
neck, her pussy feeling stretched and filled, wetter and
wetter, loud squelching sounds, Alex licking her ear and
nipping the lobe of it, a trick which sent an odd cramping
spasm through her womb, and she shivered all over: not
yet, not yet, I feel so good I don't want to come just yet,
want to go on feeling it, all of it, skin against skin, a pinch
here, a bite there, and that lovely fucking, deeper and
deeper. Fill me up with it lover, harder and harder … and
Paul shouted out something and powered into her, his hips
lifting her right off the bed, bumping her breasts against
Alex, the surging movements like riding a galloping
horse, and she was calling out now, "Yes! Yes! Yes!" and

her pussy convulsed, all her muscles contracted and spasmed, and she whimpered, clinging to Alex as Paul gave one final heave and spurted hot and hard inside her.

Lying between them, sipping red wine, hazy and happy in the warm peace of afterglow, Stephanie found her thoughts turning to the Tanners, and wondered what was happening right now in the lower courtyard, around the huge fire. She envisaged Jade, stripped and bound, with a lash falling repeatedly across her slender shoulders, writhing and crying in a mixture of rage and delight. She imagined Budgie surrounded by adoring women, one sucking his thick cock, another cramming full breasts into his mouth. The images appealed to her, yet her time there seemed like a dream. Still, somewhere deep inside her was a new level of awareness, a knowledge of the endless possibilities of her own sexuality, and the feeling was very fine.

"Maybe next summer I'll go back and take a look again," she murmured and Paul, drowsily moving beside her, gave her right breast a quick squeeze.

"That bikers' place?"

"Yeah. Maybe I'll buy a bike and pay them all a visit - just for a change."

"Maybe we'll come with you," Alex suggested, dropping a kiss on her left nipple.

"Or maybe if you just fancy a change, we could sort something out for you - a little weekend surprise," said Paul, and Stephanie purred with contentment as she and her two favourite people drifted happily off to sleep.

The Punishment Room had two main lights, with a dimmer switch, and one spotlight, but tonight Max had switched them all off and lit a dozen white candles, which were set in a stately, free-standing candelabra. Poppy, standing quietly in the centre of the room, her hands clasped behind her back, wore only black hold-up stockings with a wide lace band, and a pair of high-heeled black shoes, with little rings at the back of each one, through which were clipped tiny padlocks. Beside her was a display stand made of cast iron, draped with a black velvet cloth, and on the top tier, arranged on the cloth, was a collar, made of silver, hinged at one side and fastening at the other with a loop and buckle. A small silver padlock, with a glowing emerald inset on one side, lay next to the collar, and she looked at it, admiring its simple beauty. Max, dressed in black, pushed a chair towards her, the high-backed wooden chair that served a variety of purposes in this room.

"Sit down."

She obeyed, holding her body tense with expectation, her nipples already hard and tight.

"Legs apart, slut."

Again, she did as she was asked, not entirely sure where all this was leading - but the mystery, the possibility of surprise, only intensified her enjoyment of the situation. She felt a little shiver ripple through her, like a cool breeze from nowhere, as she looked up into his dark, unfathomable eyes.

"Bring yourself to orgasm. You have thirty seconds."

The command was as emotionless as the others, yet it thrilled her deeply. Spreading her legs even further apart, she began to touch herself, holding her pussy lips apart with one hand and sliding a finger of the other into her wet, warm channel, easing it in and out and brushing the heel of her hand against her pubic mound. Almost immediately, she felt a rush of blood to her vulva, a quivering in her thighs, and she started to frig herself harder, dabbling in her juices, twirling her fingers round her clit, bringing a hand up to pull on her own nipples, twisting the little buds hard between finger and thumb.

"Orgasm, slut," came the voice of her master, and Poppy jerked in her chair and came, rocking back and forth and gasping loudly. Moving round to stand behind her, Max placed his hands on her shoulders and kissed her temple.

"That was your last orgasm as a free woman," he whispered. "Unless you choose to change your mind. You have three choices, slut. You can accept the collar, as a visible sign that you belong to me, you can leave, now and forever … or you can stay, unmarked. Choose now."

Poppy felt tears well up, though they did not fall. She didn't want to cry yet, and indeed, she was happy, not sad. The core, if not the actual form of this ritual had been her choice, her atonement, and she took a gut-deep pleasure in every step his imagination led her on. Had he ever let her down? She tried and failed to regulate her breathing, and knew her voice was unsteady when she replied.

"I accept the collar. I want to wear it, Master."

He placed the cold metal round her neck, and it felt smooth, not too heavy, but heavy enough that she would never be able to forget that she was wearing it. He put the padlock through the loop of the buckle, and closed it with a tiny snicking sound. Then, out of a pocket of his black trousers, he produced a small silver key, and unlocked it again. Poppy wanted to protest, to plead, but made herself keep silent; Max was teasing her, if only a very little. He turned the key and locked her into the collar again, and there was a heavy silence in the candlelit room.

"Very well …" Max said, and she felt his pride in her, his satisfaction, and juices bubbled between her thighs again.

He bent to the display stand and, from a lower shelf under the black velvet drape, he produced a small metal block, and laid the key in the centre of it before reaching behind the cloth again and bringing out an ordinary club hammer.

"Watch carefully, little one," he murmured, and brought the hammer crashing down on the key. Four separate times he brought it down, four loudly-ringing blows, until the key was destroyed, a misshapen mess.

"That is the only key. Now you are irrevocably locked, irrevocably bonded, irrevocably mine. Get up."

Poppy got to her feet, the sound of the hammer-strikes still echoing in her head, and followed his pointing finger to the cross against the wall.

"Face me," he said, and tied her to it, her back against the cool metal, her legs wide apart. He took a small, slender black vibrator and slipped it into her dripping pussy, switching it on so that it buzzed, loudly, sending shock waves through her already engorged and swollen clitoris.

"Now wait," he commanded, and moved away into the shadows. Poppy clenched her quim muscles round the jittering plastic tube, not sure if she had been given permission to come or not. She tried to hold back, just in case, but the constant throbbing, the harsh tickling feeling, was too powerful to resist, and she came, body shuddering, head tossing from side to side. She tried to expel the vibrator, but was unable to get sufficient purchase with her muscles, and it had driven her to another orgasm by the time Max came back, naked and erect.

He said nothing, but tugged the humming dildo roughly out of her vagina and pushed himself inside her in its place. He took her without speaking, without touching her breasts, and came quickly, sliding out of her and stepping back. Only then did he address her again.

"Tonight I'm going to make use of each one of your orifices, Poppy. That was only the first one. I am going to use your body for my pleasure, mark you and punish you and teach you and abuse you. If you thought that putting my collar around your neck was a simple matter, you were wrong."

He hadn't given her permission to speak, so Poppy kept her mouth shut, feeling his seed inside her, beginning to trickle down her legs, and writhing a little with the exquisite blend of pleasure achieved and pleasure anticipated.

Max showed her a pack of ordinary wooden clothes pegs, and she flinched, looking at the cruel curve of his smile. She hated clothes pegs, and he knew it.

He fastened one on each nipple, bringing little squeals of protest from her, and then one on her lower lip, which made her wail miserably. Finally, crouching at her feet, he held her labia apart and clipped three pegs onto each soft, fleshy lip. Poppy screamed a couple of times, then lapsed into a series of hoarse, loud grunts. Each peg was a separate source of pain, like a live flame, eating into her flesh, and she shivered and sweated, squirming in her bondage, loving and hating every long second simultaneously.

Max had taken several steps away and now stood watching her as she twisted and strained her body in her distress. Eventually, he uncoiled the long whip that he held, twirled it once and cracked it, neatly removing the peg from her left nipple. She shouted as the new pain overrode the old, shouted louder as he whipped the peg away from her right breast, and when the whip cracked between her legs she howled like a banshee as the clothes pegs clattered to the floor. She opened her eyes, blinking away tears, and saw that his cock had stiffened once more, and the pain seemed to dwindle like a light going out.

He waited until she was quiet again, and undid the cuffs that bound her, taking her to the whipping stool and bending her over it, face down. She thought he would tie her again, but he held her bottom open, smeared her with some greasy substance and began to slide his member into her anal opening, and she bore down eagerly to accept him. She clutched the legs of the apparatus, feeling her pussy open and close on nothing, involuntary movements of desire, and was grateful for the sudden pressure of his finger on her clitoris, frigging her hard so that she came in sharp, rippling waves, the intense quivers of her bottom milking gouts of semen from his prick.

He tied her to the block then, once he had slithered out of her arse, and left the room. She lay there, quiescent, waiting, glowing, trembling with pleasure, wondering what he would do to her next. *Every orifice*, he had said, and she licked her lips with avidity.

The collar around her neck was a cool, noticeable weight - a living, constant reminder of Max and their bond. She belonged to him, she knew that with every fibre of herself, and yet, and yet …

She smiled in the candlelight, feeling her long red hair tumble over her face. She would run away again some time, now she knew he would follow her - and now she knew the dark delights each parting and reunion could bring. You cherish what you have all the more when it drifts from time to time right out of your reach, she thought, and then, at the sound of his returning footsteps, her lithe frame tensed, she clenched the muscles of her belly and thighs, and let herself go into another, brief but passionately deep, shuddering orgasm.

The saloon bar smelt of a curious mixture: engine oil, smoke, beer, male sweat, male pheromones, and leather. Inhaling deep lungfuls, the woman in the short, tight, black dress felt a flutter of sensation deep within her vagina, and wondered if the hardening of her small nipples was likely to be perceptible to anyone. She slipped through the crowd of bikers, keeping her head down, nervous yet exhilarated, her mind a whirl of duelling impulses: to give it up now, turn and run, to compromise, merely absorb the atmosphere, take it as fuel for the fantasies upon which her imagination would feed, alone in her bed with her fingers strumming her clitty and working in and out of her quim ... or the third, the most terrifying option, to go ahead and make herself available, open herself to the experience she both deeply feared and deeply craved.

She managed to attract the attention of the barman, and bought herself a glass of white wine. It was slightly sour, and not really cold enough, but she sipped it anyway, wedging herself in a corner between a fruit machine and a wall, eyes darting round the room, seeking and not finding at first, then unsure, then suddenly sure.

He was stocky, but he moved with remarkable light-footed grace, his expression was alert, but alert to every remote possibility of pleasure and amusement rather than fearful of aggravation. He glanced across at her, and might have glanced away, but she let her ash-blonde hair fall forward over her face, and touched her lower lip with the tip of her thumbnail, shifting her weight from left to right foot and jiggling her breasts as she did so.

Budgie was not, initially, very interested in the blonde woman standing by the fruit machine - too classy, too dull. Still, she was putting on a right flirty display there, and it was definitely him she kept looking at, and then just as quickly looking away. He rubbed a hand over his closely-clipped skull and picked up his empty glass, wandering towards her in a way that would allow him to move on nonchalantly if she didn't look worth the bother close up. When he got to within a couple of feet of her, and she shot him a quick, fluttery nervous smile, he felt a definite stirring in his crotch - she was actually very tasty indeed. Luckily, her glass was practically empty, as well, so he had his opening line without any discernible effort.

"Buy you another one of those?" A little nod of her head, and he squeezed himself in between two of his mates and bawled the order at the barman's back. Drinks in hand, he returned to the blonde, amusing himself with a fantasy about how she would look bent over a whipping block, curvy little bottom in the air.

"Don't see smart girls like you in here very often," he said genially. "What's your name then?"

"Margaret," the blonde replied. "Margaret Hughes."

And I know exactly who you are, Mr Barr, she thought to herself. That just happens to be why I'm here.

THE FOLLOWING extract is from the opening sequence of Olivia Holland's first and wonderfully erotic adventure - **The Instruction of Olivia** (purchasing details at the back of this book).

"Olivia Holland!" The court usher poked his head around the door and beckoned with his forefinger.

"Yes, you. Come along girl."

Olivia, a tall slender girl of eighteen rose wearily from the bench and followed him into the magistrates' court. Suddenly, dressed in her tattered rags and with mud spattered legs she felt very conspicuous and alone in the world. She had been chased the whole length of the High Street for stealing a loaf of bread, which, the constable assured her, was a hanging offence; already the noose seemed to tighten around her neck.

Her hand went involuntarily to the lump forming in her throat, then, conscious of the rip in her dress, she tugged the material tighter over her bosom and stared blankly at the magistrate.

"Take your hand away from there and stand up straight!" he barked, squinting his eyes in the gloom.

Olivia came to attention and the lapels fell open, revealing a bust of larger than average size, made more prominent by the slim waist beneath. Indeed, it seemed remarkable that her narrow shoulders could carry so much weight. With all eyes riveted on her bust, Olivia blushed red and knew, to her acute embarrassment, there was nothing she could do to prevent her nipples from hardening upwards, pushing at the thin cotton like young strawberries eager for the sunshine.

For a few moments the magistrate stared back. In his mind he had already undressed her and was availing himself of those ripe fruits, working his tongue all around them, sucking them raw; a stark contrast to the thin, undernourished waifs he usually sentenced.

"Stealing is a serious crime," he said, mopping his brow with a red spotted handkerchief. "A hanging offence, in fact, and normally I would have no hesitation in dispatching you thither. Do you comprehend my meaning?"

Olivia nodded. A cold sweat had broken out under her armpits and was trickling down her sides; she was sure this was to be her last day on earth. It mattered not that her nipples stiffened further or at any second her bladder would suddenly gush its contents all over the floor; here, in this dismal room, her short life was about to end.

"Stop snivelling girl, and look at me when I speak to you."

Olivia lifted her tear streaked face, and avoiding his penetrating eyes, gazed absently at the clock, watching the hands beat away her remaining minutes. They seemed to go very fast; much faster than they had when she was sat outside on the bench.

The magistrate stroked his chin thoughtfully. He had no intentions of sending such a splendid body to the gallows, or shipping it off to Australasia. She was the last case to be heard that morning, and with a whole afternoon free other ideas came to the fore.

"I am sentencing you to six months hard labour in the House of Correction. And," he added joyfully, "twenty-four strokes of the birch; half now and half on your admission. Stand down."

"I'm not being hanged, sir?" Olivia sobbed, clutching the rail for support.

"Not at all. But you will be flogged, and flogged hard, you may rest assured of that."

He watched her cross the courtroom, his eyes no less riveted on her bottom than they had been on her bust. It seemed remarkable how similar in proportion and appearance was the lower regions of her anatomy to those at the top. Her dress, two sizes too small, hugged her cheeks as she walked. The faded pattern of stripes danced with each frightened step, going into the cleft and out again, stretching over the colliding globes, and threatening to burst at any moment. He watched her out of sight and went quickly down the back stairs to the cells beneath, tripping over his gown on the way and almost braining himself in the process.

Olivia was ahead of him, and at a doorway she halted while another girl came out, clutching her bottom and sobbing bitterly.

"Twelve strokes they give me!" she exclaimed, as if in some way it were Olivia's fault. "Twelve strokes on my bare bum. The bastards!" She opened her mouth to utter another oath but was cut short by a hard shove in the small of her back.

"In here," said the constable who had sent the girl flying along the corridor.

Olivia stepped into a cell furnished only with a long low bench and a leather bucket in which the previous occupant had generously relieved herself.

"That sometimes happens," the constable remarked drily, seeing the look of curious fascination on Olivia's face as she peered at the yellow swirling liquid. "And I daresay that you will be no exception."

"I daresay you're right." The magistrate entered the cell and closed the door behind him. Seen close up and under the soft glow of a lamp, the magistrate had to admit, if only to himself, that Olivia was one of the most stunning looking young ladies he'd ever encountered. There was, he decided, a vague Oriental air about those huge almond eyes, her high cheek bones and voluptuous lips. But the most noticeable aspect was her hair; a vast, tumbling mass of raven locks, which under the lamp assumed a blueish sheen tinged with auburn. For a fleeting moment he was reminded of a picture he saw of an odalisque sprawling across a divan smoking a hookah, the expression on her face suggesting that nothing was beyond her capabilities when it came to pleasuring men ....

GEOFFREY ALLEN'S beautiful heroine, Olivia, will be returning for her second sensational adventure later this year - **Olivia and the Dulcinites**.

* * *

HERE'S AN extract from our May title - **Captivation** by Sarah Fisher.

Alex eased herself into a more comfortable position, afraid to speak. Peter turned his attention to the leather ties around her ankles and relief swept through her. It was short lived though; once he had untied the straps around her ankles, he moved away. She stretched out on the flagstones, waiting for him to come to free her hands. Instead he lifted her head and slipped a thin pillow beneath it. She started to protest but he seemed unreachable. She wanted to see his face, his eyes, but could only focus on his expensive shoes as he walked slowly past her. She felt him fold a blanket over her bruised and sated body, and then she let out a thin unhappy cry as she realised he intended to leave her there, tied to the floor.

"Peter," she sobbed, all her senses alight and afraid.

"Please, Peter. No, don't leave me here! I'll do whatever you want. Please, untie me ..."

But her cries fell on deaf ears. She heard the sound of his footfalls recede as he left the room, and seconds later she was plunged into total darkness. She screamed out at the indignity, the unfairness, and the memory of the dark insistent call of her own desire.

Finally she realised it was pointless. Peter Tourne had gone. She began to cry, aware that in her struggles to call Peter back she had dragged the blanket down off her shoulders.

Between her legs the sting of the belt still throbbed, while her sex, sopping wet and bruised, still glowed with the aftermath of her intense excitement. She lay still for a few seconds, hot tears still rolling down her cheeks, wondering whether she could untie herself. Her fingers fumbled with the thongs, but in the dark she couldn't see how or where the ties where held.

She listened to the room and the night outside. It seemed as if she were totally and utterly alone. The tears came back with a vengeance - tears of fear and tears of shame, for she knew that some part of her relished what Peter Tourne had given her, however much her rational mind denied it.

In the darkness Alex rolled over onto her side, making the joints in her shoulders scream. She tried to slide down under the blanket to keep warm. Her body protested as she felt the cold floor beneath her biting into her hips and knees. She shivered. It was going to be a long night.

Easing herself onto her back she concentrated on the stars, which were clearly visible through the skylight above, trying to take her mind off the pain and the strange dark thoughts that bubbled up again and again in her mind. Slowly, despite everything, she felt exhaustion creep over her aching body, and did not resist as she slipped into a light and fitful doze.

It was still dark when something woke Alex. Instantly she knew exactly where she was. Her body was cold, her muscles and bones aching with strain and cramps. She peered into the gloom, wondering if Peter had taken pity on her and returned to untie the straps. His name conjured up the images of her excitement and his body pressed deep inside her, but more compelling still, the memories of the belt biting into her delicate flesh.

Alex swallowed hard and listened. Close by she could hear someone moving about in the room. She licked her dry lips, struggling to find a voice.

"Peter?" she hissed into the darkness. The movement in the shadows stopped. Alex held her breath. "Who's there?" she eventually called uneasily, unable to keep the tremor out of the words.

She heard the footsteps moving closer, and then in the starlight caught the glint of dark eyes. Instinctively she drew herself up into a small tight ball. Her unknown visitor moved closer - so close that she could hear his breathing. He was excited, struggling for control.

There was the sudden flare of a match, and in the flickering light she saw the heavy features of the driver who had picked her up earlier in the day. His lips were slack and wet, his eyes bright with excitement. He lit a candle and stood it on the flagstones beside her. His face contorted into a lustful grimace as he took in the details of her vulnerability.

Alex shuddered, fearing the sickening desire in the swarthy man's eyes. He knelt at her feet, which she protectively curled up against her body, and grabbing hold of the corner of the blanket, whipped it away. Alex let out a thin, strangled squeal.

"No - no please," she whimpered, as his lecherous eyes roamed eagerly over her naked and bound body.